"I'M GOING TO WATCH YOU DIE, ROCKSON!" KILLOV EXCLAIMED.

The Doomsday Warrior looked up at the six-foot-thick slab that hung in the air micrometers from his nose.

"You'll be crushed, Rockson, but very, very slowly," Killov continued. "You'll feel every bone in your body snap and the very cells of your flesh explode."

Rock could feel the slab sinking slowly toward him. He turned his head sideways and pulled in his chest. It already hurt as the slab squashed his ear against the side of his skull. And then his skull began compressing as the death slab dropped another twentieth of an inch.

Killov was right. Rockson could see that already. Dying was going to hurt a lot.

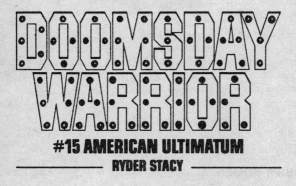

DOOMSDAY WARRIOR

#15 AMERICAN ULTIMATUM

RYDER STACY

ZEBRA BOOKS

KENSINGTON PUBLISHING CORP.

ZEBRA BOOKS

are published by

Kensington Publishing Corp.
475 Park Avenue South
New York, NY 10016

First printing: February, 1989

Printed in the United States of America

CHAPTER ONE

It was many thousands of years old, its birth lost in the dim mists of pre-history. Its face was crumbling. Dust cascaded down its granite nose, and sand swirled within its hollow deep-set eyes, which stared out only with blackness. Its long back, flanks, and legs were filled with ten thousand cracks—fissures which threatened to rip open and expose its baked innards at any moment. And yet within this decomposing physique there was a great strength, an unbreakable spirit that emanated energy. In the midst of its inevitable decomposition a ghostly voice screamed out, "I shall live forever, far beyond the lives of the men who built me, or the tens of millions who have come to see, worship, marvel over me through the centuries!"

It was called the Sphinx.

It sat in the sand, stretched like a cat, its long lion claws digging into the sand ahead of it like it was slinking, preparing for movement, perhaps ready to pounce, to leap on any who dared stare at it. It was as mysterious as the day it was chiseled, a monument to rival anything that future generations might offer the gods. A testament to the abilities of the ancient craftsmen of the Nile, and the power of the pharaohs of ancient Egypt. A colossal being sculpted out of solid rock, over 189 feet long, the massive sculpture guarded the Duqur Valley, protecting it from other gods, other men. With its human head, lion's body, and hawk's wings, it took the best of all three and combined them into one. There was something powerful in its combined characteristics, something to challenge all the other gods: the Bull God, the Cat God, even the Sun God—Amun.

In its immovable immensity and its sheer power, its magic of stone carved into myth and eternal riddle, the Sphinx seemed to toy with mankind. For the ancient myths said that the Sphinx asked a riddle of all who dared approach it.

"What walks on four feet in the morning, on two at noon, and on three in the evening?" It killed all who failed to answer the riddle, ripping them to shreds with its stone claws, its great boulder teeth. The answer was man. Man crawls as a baby in the morning of his life, walks on two feet at noon as an adult, and must use a cane in his twilight years. But none had answered the riddle. And their bones, along with the bones of the pharaoh who had built it, had been long turned to powder—the bones of all who had labored on it as well!

Yet still the great man-beast sat, asking the riddle with hollow eyes and voiceless mouth, broken mouth dug out by aeons of windswept sand which ripped into it every second of the day. It asked through a mouth which gaped wide now, dark like a cave between the smashed lips. It asked—who dares come before me and gaze directly into my eyes? Who? What man faces the impenetrable gaze of the Sphinx and thinks he will live?

In the 247th day of its 3,789th year the Sphinx

moved. Just the slightest ripple of motion at first, as if it were quivering, sending shivers along its back like a lion trying to warm itself on a cold desert night. Then it was still again as the star-studded sky looked down with its trillion eyes as if in awe of the mythical beast.

Suddenly it was vibrating wildly, every part of it shaking and jerking around as if it were going into the throes of a fit. The Sphinx, which had survived the grinding millennia, taking all that nature and man had to offer, began cracking. The face was first to go, as it crumbled apart like sand in a tidal surge. What was left of the nose cracked and slid down the face. One deep-set eye suddenly was five times larger as a whole section of the skull above it cracked with a loud snap and rushed to the desert sands below.

Suddenly all the countless tons of stone were slowly rising right up out of the desert floor, wobbling and gyrating around like a kite out of control. The immense beast rose up twenty, thirty, then fifty feet into the air. It began spinning around wildly, the long paws dipping up, then back again, like a plane which had lost its tail rudders and didn't quite know where it would head next. Then the huge stone wings which were folded back on its sides began ripping free with great cracking sounds, as if they were trying to unfurl to help it in its mad airborne fling.

As it spun around, the centrifugal force of the motion began hurling whole sections of the Great Sphinx away. The twenty-foot-long claws tore free of their boulder wrists and fell, slamming into the desert. Part of the back ripped free and exploded into pieces which showered the sand below for many yards.

The men who were standing nearby looked

terrified. The gaunt black-clad man who was causing the flying Sphinx's bodily injuries screamed out curses in a violent rage. "It sucks! This is useless! What the hell's wrong with this stinking device!" Colonel Killov, commander of what was left of the Earth's KGB forces, screamed out. The red-robed high priest of Amun stood frozen in terror at his right. "You said this powerstick could levitate anything," Killov complained. "But this damn Sphinx is just dashing itself to pieces."

"P-Perhaps Your Godship is not quite using the Qu'ul stick c-correctly," the priest, Aka-ta-Kal, offered. His white, jewel-fringed robe was now coated with ancient stone dust and sand from the Sphinx's tumbling. Aka-ta-Kal shouted his words above the din, staring with fear-swollen eyes, knowing how enraged the emaciated, drug-crazed Killov could get. The high priest had discovered this Kil-Lov who was also called Ka Amun, the son of the Great Amun. Kil-Lov had fallen from the sky, his shoes flaming and smoking—as was prophesied in the Egyptian Book of the Dead. So Head Priest Aka-ta-Kal, and all the followers of the Amun Sun God cult who lived along the upper Nile, had come to serve the Ka Amun. For the Man-God had dropped to Earth to deliver his divine message straight to their worthless ears. That's why the high priest had led the Man-God to the ancient storehouse beneath the Pyramid where he had found the Qu'ul stick.

"What the hell do you mean?" Killov screamed out, shaking his hand-held levitation device. The Qu'ul was a crudely finished red crystal in a rough cylinder shape about a foot long and three inches wide. It gave off a glow as if alive inside, as if a million burning fireflies had been trapped within its crystalline surface. As Killov angrily shook the weapon—

8

which shot out an almost invisible purple-hued beam—it lost its contact with the side of the great stone monument. The Sphinx instantly came flying straight down, a good two-hundred-foot drop. As the dozen or so Egyptian priests of the high orders of the Amun cult stood in a trembling circle around Kil-Lov the Ka Amun, they gasped collectively in abject horror as they saw the Great Sphinx smash into the side of one of the pyramids that stood below it.

There was a tremendous roar as if a burst of thunder had gone off right in front of them, and they were all showered with a blinding cloud of dust. The Sphinx had smashed into innumerable pieces against the pyramid. Every part of it had exploded out in all directions, from boulder-sized pieces to grains of sand. What had lasted aeons had been taken out of existence in an instant.

The Sphinx was dead. It was but sand for a sandbox—if there had been such things in the year 2096 A.D.

"Ah, this stupid thing is broken," Killov raged, throwing the levitation stick, the Qu'ul, to the sand.

The priests gasped again and closed their eyes reflexively for a few seconds. The dropped levitation device easily could have fallen pointing at them. But it had turned off abruptly as it left Killov's grip. For the Amun Stick needed the touch of a human being, the warmth of his circulating blood to bring it to life. And as cold as Killov's skin was, there was enough warmth to power the Qu'ul.

Gingerly Aka-ta-Kal reached down and picked the device up again, letting his own pounding heart settle. The Great Sphinx had been destroyed, just like that. It was terrible, a blasphemy. And yet—and yet—if this was what the Man-God, the Ka Amun Sky Being Kil-Lov, who had dropped from the clouds with flaming feet, wanted, such must be.

"Ka Amun," Aka-ta-Kal addressed Killov as softly as he could through the settling dust and sandstorm created by the exploding Sphinx. "Perhaps I can demonstrate the use of the Qu'ul again. It must be gripped softly and held very still, like this." The high priest held it up in front of Killov.

The KGB colonel stared at him, his whole face and body trembling. He wanted to strike out and kill those who had seen him not know how to use the power of the thing properly. For power was all to Colonel Killov, and no one could ever question his authority. But Killov wanted to learn the use of the Qu'ul levitation device even more. For he had plans, great and terrible plans, for it. Deeds to rival the most cruel of the ancient pharaohs would soon be afoot. And so he watched. And learned. He practiced with the awesome weapon that no one had dared to pick up since the days of the pharaohs—the device that had been kept hidden for thousands of years by the cultists who thought he was a god!

CHAPTER TWO

The African village that called itself Boswandi, meaning "We Who Live by the Volcano," woke early that morning. It was an important day, the most important for as long as any man in the tribe could remember. For the chief's son, Musubwambi, was to marry Unam, the daughter of the chief of the neighboring village. It was an event of profound importance to both villages since it meant they could stop the ceaseless warring that had continued between them for many years. The marriage meant that cattle would no longer be stolen, homes no longer burned, members of each tribe no longer killed as they went to gather fruits from the nearby forest or water from the rivers, or as they hunted on the plains. It meant—peace. So they all hoped.

Masdouri M'Bekwani awoke earlier than the others. He was the witch doctor of the village, which meant great and profound responsibilities for him. For his spells, incantations, potions, and sacrifices to the cattle and lion gods could well mean the difference between success and failure for this union of the two neighboring villages. They had lived in war for nearly a hundred years, since the Great Nuke

War itself had sent fire over all the continents. This section of the northern Sudan had been spared the atomic fires, which meant that the savannahs still grew, the game animals still grazed. Life could have been decent enough—if the two tribes hadn't begun warring with one another. They had been warring for a century, and would be heading into the second century within another year. To this day Masdouri didn't really understand why they fought, had always fought. Both tribes were of the same blood, had shared common beliefs and culture. Even their jewelry and the ritual tattoos and scars that they carved on their arms and chest were very similar in design and appearance. But all the similarities and friendship were lost in the spilt blood that had followed the decades immediately after the Great Fire War. The mushroom clouds had gone up as close as a hundred miles from the spot where Masdouri's thatched-roof, mud-walled hut now stood. Not that he had seen the towering funnels of glowing death. But his father had been told stories of them by *his* father. And all the secrets—of history and magic—had been passed on from generation to generation, too, with those stories.

Masdouri had no illusions. He knew that the union of the two tribes was fragile from the start. Very fragile, as brittle as the egg of an Ambala bird, which could shatter at a man's touch. The people of his tribe prayed for peace, longed for peace. For many young men had died over the years. Not a family was untouched, unscathed. Not a mother had not lost a son. And Masdouri as well—he longed for peace too. Prayed that its time had come like the great migrating herds returning to the Rift Valley year after year.

He was old now, nearly eighty, an ancient age for a

village in which fifty was considered old, sixty the blessing of the gods. Disease, attack by man and animal—all took their toll. But being so old, he had the wisdom of many years. Masdouri had seen it all.

Masdouri had been as warlike as the most hawkish of them in his youth, screaming and chanting around the fires in his most terrifying, demon-killing costumes to help the warriors get up their courage to go out and kill some more. But now things were different. Now he no longer had those feelings. Growing old takes some of the fierceness out of even the witch doctor and war-speller of the tribe. The desire for peace comes through wisdom. The desire for harmony comes through viewing too much bloodshed. Such a wise man was Masdouri. He had seen enough of the color red, enough rivers of tears from the wives and children of the dead. For such things alone man was not put on earth!

And so he felt fear. Fear of a kind he hadn't experienced for many years. He felt his very body trembling, his hands shaking as he sat up from his straw mat feeling the sweat pouring down his spindly arms and legs. For Masdouri knew that the very future of the tribe, its very existence, depended on what he did today, on whether or not he pleased the gods, carried out the right spells, picked the right potions to ward off demons and demon lackeys. And it made his heart beat like the dancing drums to have such a responsibility.

Masdouri rose slowly from the mat bed on the floor of his round mud-walled hut with finely meshed roof of vine and savannah growth. He really didn't want to get up today. Masdouri wanted to stay in the protective dimness of the klut, stay here where only a few streaks of early violet dawn broke through hair-thin cracks in the thatched roof. He felt strange

13

inside. As if there was something beyond the wedding itself, something beyond the entry into the village of many warriors from the other tribe to threaten him. Something gnawed at his very heart, tugged at it, as if trying to tell him something.

"Ah, Masdouri, you are becoming an old hen, like a woman," he scolded himself, forcing an insincere chuckle out of his narrow leathery lips. He sat fully up on the mat, his back against the rough mud and cattle-dung walls now baked hard as brick.

Father Sun had not even climbed from his black bed, and the air was thick, thicker than usual with a sheet of dank air from the jungles to the east. That didn't usually penetrate out onto the edges of the savannah belt where Masdouri and his people lived! It was going to be very hot today, he could tell already.

The gods were toying with him. They were not going to make things easy. Usually he had one of his four wives prepare his morning rituals, bring him water, but he had banished them from the klut two days before. No women could be near him for at least forty-eight hours before an important ceremony, particularly one of the magnitude of the chief's son's wedding.

This was the most important spell-dispensing he had ever undertaken. He wished he were a younger man, one with the exuberance and cockiness of youth. He felt tired, old, hardly able to rise up without the women around to fetch things for him, help him dress. He had gotten used to them. Too used to them perhaps.

Hearing his knees cracking like dry twigs, Masdouri dragged himself upright, pushing his back against one of the wooden support branches which held his klut upright.

The hardest part was getting to a standing position. Once he was fully up, it wasn't really that bad. He held onto the center support, nearly two feet thick, gnarled and twisted, and walked around it in a stumbling circle. Three times to the east, three times to the west, just to make sure that the whole wedding list of gods and devils was honored properly, making little bows at every step and mumbling prayers very fast under his breath.

Then he stopped and kindled a fire off to one side of the klut in a dugout pit. It flamed quickly. He was quite adept at such things, having been around so long. He put a gourd over it—blackened and smeared with pitch on the bottom so it could take heat without cracking—and heated up his morning drink, Kusamba, a mixture of cattle blood, curdled milk, and herbs. It tasted wonderful and energizing. After he had finished the Kusamba he felt more awake and alert.

Masdouri surveyed the curved walls of the klut, looking at the numerous masks, costumes, rattles, and other sacred items which only he knew and understood the significance of. The main question was just what he would wear today. It had been bothering him for weeks. There were no real rules about intertribal marriages, because there hadn't been one in his time—or even that of his father, who had taught him all that he knew about the magic ways. He had put off the decision about what to wear. Now the morning of the Day was here, and he still wasn't sure at all.

Hmmm! Let's see. The lion mask for sure, with its actual lion's face, a big male with thick golden mane and jaws that looked like they could swallow a man whole. It was a creature he himself had killed many years before. It was a little tattered by now, slightly diminished in the luster of its fur, but not in its fierce pride.

Yes, the lion's mask, that was for sure. It was the only headpiece that he felt was strong enough to ward off supernatural attacks. And for his body, why not the serpent outfit, with its overlaid black-bark scales so that it looked almost snakelike, sinuous when he moved. Yes, that would contrast frighteningly with the lion's head. The snake and the lion were compatible as well in divine tradition. For it was not just the guests he wished to impress—but the animal gods and the plains weather gods as well. There were many, many things to consider.

But like a crack of lightning on the savannah horizon, it all seemed so clear on this burning morning. He smiled as he reached up onto the mud wall to take down what he would wear today. In his chest it felt right. And that was where he always looked for the final decision. To the heart.

Once he was fully outfitted, he headed outside. But Masdouri reeled as he stepped into the rays of the fully risen sun. He would have to wear the heavy and hot costume all day! He could not be seen even for one instant as Masdouri by the others, not on this day. He was now the Lion Man, maker and breaker of souls—let all fear the Lion Man. And even though they knew who he was, all of the tribe—the children running naked through the village between the scores of kluts, the bare-breasted women adorning themselves with their beads, shells, ostrich feathers, and precious stones—they would all fear to look toward Masdouri. Today, he was of the gods, not of men.

Masdouri spent the day preparing for the cere-

16

monies. There were the twin fires to build—one to ward off demons, the other to welcome, to warm the lion gods when they came to witness the marriage in the cool evening. As well, Masdouri had to plant stakes in the ground all around the ritual fires in a circle nearly a hundred feet in diameter. Within this circle the dancing and the wedding would take place. He couldn't have possibly done it all on his own, but he had three apprentice-boys, one of whom would someday be his heir.

Tradition had it that the witch doctor passed his position to his firstborn son, but Masdouri had been cursed by the plains gods in that respect. Though he had tried with over a dozen wives over the years, he had never produced offspring. Thus he would choose one of the three teens to take his place; he still wasn't sure which one. All were intelligent, quick to do his bidding. He kept his eye on all of them, particularly on such a day as this.

At last it was all done, and the sun began sinking again, the evening breezes slinking along the savannah which surrounded the grove of cooling trees within which the village had been built. The log and zebra-skin drums began pounding. The men danced wildly around the fires in their own elaborate outfits of bones, feathers, and lion and cheetah hides. Many of them were already somewhat drunk from the Dsaka leaves which they had buried in large gourds the month before. Now the juices within the leaves had fermented and were potent. The leaves burned the tongue, made the body loose and the mind festive.

The sun had disappeared completely, like a snake back into its hole for the night, when they all heard a commotion coming across the black-shadowed savannah.

17

The Triori. They were here.

Instantly, all the men in the tribe tensed up, and Masdouri could see they were nervous. Weapons, spears, battle swords had all been put away, but were close at hand just in case there was trouble. It was up to him to see that there wasn't. He shook his hummingbird-bones rattle and jumped around wildly, catching their attention as the king of the Triori was carried in on a leopard sedan by ten warriors, lions' teeth covering his round chest and stomach. Behind him came the princess, carried along as well. She was beautiful, and the women stared jealously, the men lustfully, as she was brought in and set down within the magic circle alongside her father.

The chief of his tribe greeted the chief of the Triori with all the friendliness of a brother. Both men wanted this peace, this marriage. They had met twice, secretly, over the last year to make it happen. And a genuine warmth had somehow sprung up between the two. He greeted the Triori wearing his own crocodile costume, the Triori in water-buffalo garb, with huge horns fitted on top of the elaborate headdress he carried. The two men embraced, and the crowds of both tribes cheered.

The chief's son stood by his side and looked fixedly at his bride-to-be, who returned his glances with coy, quick looks of her own. They had not met before. All had been arranged by their fathers. But when they saw each other, they were not unhappy. There was, Masdouri felt, an instant attraction between them.

"Come, let us drink like elephants, eat like lions, and dance like ostriches in heat," Masdouri's chief said, leading the Triori chief to an honored seat by his throne. A second throne had been constructed just for his visit. The other chief's chair was a bit smaller than his own, but nonetheless it was festooned with skins and teeth quite worthy of any chieftain.

The two groups of warriors didn't mingle, but stood on opposite sides of the circle of magic that Masdouri had built and looked at each other nervously. There had been too much fighting and death over the years for them to relax so easily. But they tried. Their kings, after all, had decreed that the time for peace was here. One did not argue with the chief.

With log drums pounding out steady and nearly deafening beats, the two tribes began dancing wildly as they consumed the leaf-liquor. Now that they weren't fighting, the men of the tribes tried to compete in dance—their leaps, the speed of their turns, the believability of the animals they imitated. The dancing grew frenzied as the women performed their own steps just outside the magic circle.

At last the wedding was at hand, and they all gathered together in the center of the circle as Masdouri, with the other tribe's witch man by his side, began performing the sacred rituals. First, the sacrifice of two cattle, one from each tribe, their throats slit, so the blood of both ran together in a puddle. Then, taking the blood from the still-pulsing wounds and filling cups with it. Then the actual uniting of the man and his bride. The two stood side by side as Masdouri mouthed the sacred words of union: "Be proud before the gods, for blood and rank are thine, and—" He was halfway through the ceremony when suddenly there was a tremendous thunder from the north. All motion ceased as he stopped speaking. His hand froze as it held the rattle.

For a moment all suspected treachery, and he could see the warriors of both tribes were wondering whether to reach for their hidden weapons.

Suddenly the sounds came again and they were much louder this time. It was as if the light-waterfalls of the storms that swept over the village during the rainy season had descended to the very earth. For they could all feel the earth trembling beneath their feet, shaking their sweaty bodies. Some of the women began screaming, and suddenly Masdouri saw it, whatever it was, coming toward them. It was large, impossibly large, a mountain dropping from the sky. He thought for a moment that he had gone mad or had consumed too much of the burning leaf-liquor. Mountains did not drop from the clouds!

And yet—it was a mountain. A solid object that was larger than their whole village. It was rising up perhaps a hundred feet into the air, and then slamming down again, sending up great clouds of dust. And it was coming right toward them. An impossible, village-sized, bouncing ball of death!

Pandemonium broke out as warriors and women began running in all directions, not even sure which way to go. Suddenly Masdouri realized he was standing stupidly in the center of the magic circle by himself. The ball-mountain was coming straight for their village, only a half mile or so off, and even as he watched he could see it fall, rise up again, and move forward another hundred yards. And where it rose, all that had been beneath it was crushed, squashed. Trees, bushes, animals, nothing was spared, all ground down to a bloody pulp of dust and powdered bone.

Not knowing where to run himself, Masdouri headed toward his klut. Making his old bones push him forward at a run, he dove through the gazelle-hide door flap and collapsed onto his knees breathing hard.

He had failed. The gods were not pleased with

what he had done. Or was it the gods? He had never seen them angry like this. But he knew one thing—he was about to die. Sighing, he rose and walked over to his meditation chair, a zebra-skin stool. Masdouri sat cross-legged on it. He did not really mind dying, for he was old. But he minded very much that he might have done something wrong. He sat there, uttering chants, yelling out as fast as he knew how every demon-destroyer chant in his repertoire. But it seemed to do nothing as the thunder-explosions grew closer by the second, making the earth shake as if in the throes of a full-scale earthquake.

He didn't see the rest of the villagers get crushed like so many ants as the mountain-ball came down just fifty feet short of his klut. But he knew they were dead. He could feel the souls depart en masse. He heard a whooshing sound as though a vacuum had suddenly been created and was filling with a snap of air as the mountain rose up again overhead.

Masdouri knew it was overhead, right overhead. He could sense its immense crushing weight. And he sent out a final burst of prayer to the gods, all the gods, and hoped they would take him in. He had been a good man. He had tried. Tried to bring peace. And suddenly it occurred to him: Perhaps the gods didn't want peace.

Then the mountain came down and he was no more. Masdouri was turned into a red gruel which mixed with his lifetime of costumes and masks, the mud walls of his klut, and the very earth itself. All was mixed into a swamp of death.

Eight thousand miles away in Moscow, in a Kremlin bedroom overlooking Red Square, Rahallah, Son of the Plains Lion, a witch doctor in his own right,

21

CHAPTER THREE

The two men stood frozen, facing each other six feet apart. Their eyes were focused on one another like those of two panthers, locked in a hard cool gaze, the gaze of the predator, the stalker, the killer. Both were stopped in time, every muscle locked. They were coiled tightly as springs ready to move, to give motion to their potential energy at any moment. They saw without looking, heard without listening for the slightest sound of bone creaking, or sudden intake of breath. Both took in all the information that the other man was sending out, without words. For both were perfect fighting machines and had no need to posture or make threatening gestures. They were beyond that, far beyond that. They were Zen practitioners of the art of hand-to-hand combat. Warriors beyond the ken of most men.

Suddenly one of them, the smaller one, an Oriental man with almond eyes and dark mustache, moved with the blinding speed of a cobra striking. Only the slightest flap of his neck-to-ankles black ninja suit, loosely gathered around him, betrayed motion. But it was enough for the taller and stockier man, dressed in combat fatigues and sweatshirt, to sense the attack.

23

He turned his hips just slightly to meet the blurred attack of the Oriental. Barely. For even as he turned, he felt the rising foot of the attacker slam into his chest and spin him sideways. Only the fact that he had already shifted enabled him to take the brunt of the attack without going down. Even as the Oriental's fists came flying in toward his face, like hawks diving for prey, he was able to grab hold of the leg that had just kicked him. Turning his hips a notch more, he sent the man flying over on his side.

The motion knocked both of them backwards, yet even as they hit the wooden floor both came up on a roll quicker than the eye could see. A thin smile crossed the Asian's face and the word "good" seemed to float across his mouth, as if he were pleased to have such an opponent. The bigger man grinned as well, but only for an instant. For even as he did, he saw that the Oriental was coming at him with what seemed like an impossible speed from just a few feet off. Even as he raised both hands preparing to meet the attack, the Oriental leaped right off the ground like a Harrier jet fighter—which can take off vertically. High jump kicks, it has always been said by martial-arts devotees, are dangerous—because they take both of the jumper's legs off the ground and he's most vulnerable at that moment. But that warning applied to *normal* men's kicks. This man was not normal.

But the larger man knew that, and even as he saw the double kick coming in, his mismatched aqua and violet eyes twinkled with a gleam. For he had known, had sensed that that was what the Oriental was about to try. He ducked down. Simple as that. The kicker flew right overhead and as he passed by, the larger man reached up and grabbed hold of one of the slightly flapping black ankle pants, pulling hard. The Oriental slammed down to the floor, yet somehow he hit in a ball shape and merely rolled over twice. Then he was on his feet again even as his adversary came charging in with his own attack.

He came in fast, punching out a series of snapping fists that would have made a cobra blink in amazement at the sheer speed of the punches. One of them made contact, barely, with the chest of the smaller man, but the rest were blocked, knocked away with what seemed like the lightest of slaps, as if the Oriental's hands were small windmills and he was swatting out at flies. Suddenly—and the larger man had no idea how really, for he saw nothing move on the Oriental —he was being tripped. His ankles were all locked up, as if there were ropes around him. And even as he toppled over like an old tree, he glanced down to see that somehow the Oriental had unwrapped the black silk belt from around his waist and thrown it down around the knees of his opponent.

"You son of a bitch, that's cheating," Ted Rockson bellowed, even as he threw out both hands to soften his fall onto the hard wooden floor.

"All's fair in love and combat," Chen chortled, as he jumped right over the falling man and landed with both legs spread on each side of the sprawled Freefighter's back. He raised one foot as if preparing to bring it down onto the spinal cord and take his opponent out once and for all.

Suddenly a scream rent the air that made both men stop in their tracks and their eyes dart over to the side. A buxom red headed woman clad in skintight pink leotards was holding her hands half over her eyes.

"Stop! Stop! You'll kill him with a blow like that," Rona wailed, starting forward ready to dive into the fray.

"You mean a blow like this?" Chen laughed, bringing the leg down hard so that his foot slammed

25

into the floor about six inches from Ted Rockson's right ear. "I think it might only hurt the floor." He laughed as he reached down and gripped his sash, pulling it free from the entangling knot it had formed around Rockson's knees.

"You sly devil," Rock said as he rose to his feet, Chen helping him up with one hand. "I gotta keep my eye on you every second when we spar, I'll damn well tell you that."

"That's the whole idea, isn't it, Rock?" Chen grinned back, wrapping the sash back around his waist. "You and I spar to teach each other new things. Otherwise, what would be the point? Both of us can take out most men. This is a chance to really test each other. I've been toying with this bolo idea for a while. See, it has little weights at each end of the sash. I've taken down deer and elk on hunting trips recently. Just wanted to see if it would work on someone like you. It does."

"Oh, Rock, are you all right?" Rona Wallender said as she rushed over to the Doomsday Warrior, running her hands around his bare muscular shoulders and chest like a cop frisking a suspect. "You might . . . have gotten hurt." She looked horrified by the thought of anything happening to the only man she had ever been able to really feel something for. Which was a little absurd, as he had faced mutants, Red search-and-destroy squads, and far worse for most of his life. "Rock" had managed to survive for the last twenty-five years since he had wandered into Century City as a teenager after his family had been killed by a roving band of KGB'ers.

"I think perhaps the opposite might have been the case," Chen muttered with a twinkle in his brown eyes. "I think perhaps you didn't see Rock's foot ready to drive up into my—um—private areas—had I

26

continued any closer with my kick. But Rock, let's try it again. Now that you know what I'll be doing—see if you can counter it, okay? I'm not giving any clues—but there is a simple enough way."

"Oh, you men," Rona huffed as she stepped back. Rockson was inside the subterranean walls of Century City rarely enough these days, and she could hardly stand the thought that he would not spend it all with her. And yet his very stubbornness was one of the things that drew her to him. That and the fact that she could kick the butt of just about every other man in CC—except for the two in front of her! Well, perhaps a few others of Rock's inner elite team of wasteland commandos could give her a hard time.

For better or worse, Rona was the type of woman who couldn't sleep with a man if she could beat him up.

"Sure, let's try it again," Rock said, gently extricating himself from the red-haired beauty's clutching grip. "The next man who tries something like that on me might not be friendly." They squared off and went at it once more. Chen didn't take the sash off right away, preferring to wait until Rockson wasn't expecting it. But after several minutes of back-and-forth punching, kicking, flipping, and rolling, using maneuvers from about a dozen different fighting arts, Rock started forward. He had just managed to flip Chen with an Aiki-Jitsu move when he saw the sash come off fast. Before he could move, Chen had snapped it out toward his legs. But Rock had been figuring just how he would respond on the next try. He leaped high in the air, as if jumping rope, as the makeshift bolo came spinning at him. It missed this time, but kept going and managed to wrap itself twice right around Rona's curvy hips. She yelled out, "I dislike this intensely!"

27

"I think it likes you, sugar," Rockson said as he slammed Chen down onto the gym floor.

"Good move, Rock," Chen said as the two men stopped their sparring. The Chinese-American head instructor of all Century City hand-to-hand combat courses slapped Rock on the shoulder. "There are three or four ways to avoid it as far as I can figure— but that's probably the easiest—unless, of course, I had thrown higher."

"Oh, you two," Rona said with disgust as she unwrapped the silk snake from around her mid-section. "Fight, fight, fight. Is that all you two macho men can talk about?"

"No, we talk about the weather sometimes, too," Chen said mockingly. All three pairs of eyes suddenly turned to the right, looking past the groups of other men and women working out on mats all around the exercise and martial-arts training level, just one of many that made up CC's underground city. One of Rath's Intelligence people—by the color of his lapels—was tearing down the gymnasium floor toward the three of them.

"Whoa, pardner, easy," Rock said as the huffing and puffing fellow, clearly a little overweight to judge by the bulge under his shirt and the red flush on his face, came to a halt. "Don't want to get a stroke before you hit thirty."

"Sorry, sir, sorry," the man said, snapping up to a salute. He then became even more flushed. He knew Ted Rockson—even though he was the military commander of CC, even though he was known as the Doomsday Warrior, whose name alone meant hope to the downtrodden slave masses throughout America—didn't like salutes. Rock didn't like any of that military bull. Rockson was famous for his dislike of all trappings of glory.

28

"Spit it out, mister," Rona demanded impatiently.

"Rath sent me to contact you, Rock. All our internal intercom lines are still out, so . . . There's a message coming in on several telecom frequencies. Keeps calling your name, then goes into some weird code that the cipher boys can't even begin to make heads or tails of. And it's coming, as far as we can backtrack it from its satellite bounce, all the way from Moscow. Rath said I should bring you right back to the comm room, see if you can make anything of it."

"I'll see you later," Rockson said, slapping Chen on the chest. "Good workout. But let me have one of those bolo belts next time—see if I can lasso you." The Chinese American just grinned silently.

Rock turned to Rona. "I'll see you later, baby. I think we have an appointment for this evening." It was Rona's birthday and Rockson had promised, absolutely promised, that Russian MIGs couldn't drag him away from this. He had missed the last three of the redhead's birthdays while out on combat duty.

"You miss it and you're in big trouble, mister," the fiery beauty said, her cheeks reddening to nearly the color of her mane of hair, which cascaded down her shoulders to her slim waist. "I don't care if Premier Vassily himself wants to surrender the Red Empire to you lock, stock, and barrel! My birthday dinner comes first."

"Start powdering your nose, baby," Rock commented. "You know I'm more scared of you than the whole damned Red Army. I'll meet you at the Sky Lounge at, say"—he checked a wall clock—"six-thirty." With that he turned and started double timing along with the huffing messenger back across the exercise level.

There were over twenty levels of the underground

29

Century City, an entire subterranean city of Free-fighting men, women, and children buried in the Rocky Mountains. Each level specialized in a different function: living cubes, commissaries, a hospital, libraries, and armaments factories which turned out the Liberator Rifle, SMG, and various other military weapons which were shipped out to other Freefighting cities around America. Century City had been founded by highway commuters who had gotten trapped inside an interstate tunnel complex when World War III had begun over a century earlier. It was a far different place now, with its multiple levels and functions and over 50,000 inhabitants, than it had been then. Rock was always impressed with the ever-advancing city when he moved through it.

Still, even though it was the most advanced of all the guerrilla cities, not everything always functioned quite as it should. Although there was an elevator system which could carry a man in seconds to any of the complex's levels, it wasn't functioning right now. A recent disturbance in the thermal heat ducts which the city used to partially power itself had sent up geysers of superheated steam right into the main power circuits for the lift system. So the whole Freefighter city had to use the walk ramps which, thank God, had been built many decades earlier— way before the city even had elevators or moving walkways. Men and women were pushing carts up and down the ramps, and using small vehicles to carry supplies back and forth around the city. Its vital functions couldn't stop even for a day. Not if America was to triumph over the Reds.

It was clearly hard work for the messenger, who was so red faced by the time they reached Intel Chief Rath's main war room that Rockson ordered the guy to sit down and take a breather.

"Should really get your men into better shape, Rath," Rockson said as the dour hawk-nosed Rath paced impatiently around a table filled with men monitoring radios and satellite frequencies. Rock knew they were there twenty-four hours a day, trying to increase their information on Russian troop movements, convoys, and other intel.

"Right, Rockson. I'll take all my men off their command posts and have them jog five times around the city." He said it without the trace of a smile. The two men had had their differences many times, but they had to work together.

"So what's the emergency?" Rock asked with his own scowl. He would have vastly preferred working out with Chen for another hour than playing around with Intel Chief Rath.

"We've been getting a repeated message being played over half the Red intercontinental-transmissions comm satellites. It begins with your name, and then goes right into a code that none of us have heard before. The Reds aren't the greatest cryptics experts, so we can't figure out how they developed this one—and why they're so damned impatient to get this info to you. Here, listen." Rath flipped a switch on one of the comm units that filled a long metal table, and immediately a voice came over the speakers that were mounted up on the walls.

"17, numbers 3, 9, 15, 27, 89, 121, 189. 19, numbers 11, 17, 84, 87, 99, 122, 143, 155. 347—"

"What the hell is it?" Rath blurted out after a few seconds. "Do you know?"

Rockson looked confused as well as he tried to zero in on the voice that was reciting the numbers. It was a deep basso voice that read off the "meaningless" numbers.

31

"You say this is coming from Russia? From what city, comrade?" Rock asked with a smirk. Rath's mouth didn't budge a millimeter.

"Moscow, or very close to it, as far as we can tell. Do you have any idea what—"

"Yeah, I think I do," Rock replied. "Have one of your men run to the library and pick up a copy of *War and Peace*. I pray we have a copy."

"*War and Peace*? What the hell are you talking about?" Rath exclaimed, flustered, wondering if Rockson had finally cracked up.

"The speaker on that tape is Rahallah, Premier Vassily's right-hand man," Rock said softly, starting to realize that something really was up if the African was putting so much effort and using all their comm lines to get to him. "When I was in Moscow we worked out an arrangment that if either of us had to contact the other and didn't want anyone else to know about it, we would use *War and Peace* as our code framework. The first number of each sequence is the page; the following numbers are the words on that page. It's a childishly simple code system. But if you don't know what book it refers to, you could spend the rest of your days trying to figure the damned thing out."

Rath looked stunned for some reason, perhaps because he had had his entire operations unit spend hours trying to figure the thing out. "But I'm afraid that if it's Rahallah calling," Rock said almost in a whisper, "the message can only concern war. Men don't get that desperate when their words are of peace."

CHAPTER FOUR

But it wasn't going to be as easy as that. Rockson had learned long ago that nothing is. One of Rath's intel ops ran down to the Century City library, and after scrounging around for nearly half an hour was able to find a dog-eared copy of the novel—somewhat motheaten, to say the least, pages yellowed as corn. But the words, which were what mattered, were all still there. However, when it was brought back and they began trying to decipher the code that Rahallah and Rock had worked out, the cipher boys ran into problems. The very first part of the message appeared to read, when translated, "Tree love no samovar quick Czar appetite dirt dog." So much for the first sentence, which Rock thought might have been some form of beatnik poetry circa the mid-twentieth century, but hardly a decoded emergency message from the Kremlin!

"The problem is—we've got different editions of the book in English," Rath suddenly exclaimed, slapping his forehead with such force that it looked like it hurt. "Even slight differences in the number of words per page makes it all not match up." He thought for a few more seconds, his brain whirring feverishly, his eyes half closed as he was wont to do when deep in concentration. Even Rockson had to admit, though there were plenty of things he didn't like about the man, he did his job well, almost fanatically.

"But we will be able to figure it out anyway," the intel chief suddenly blurted out as his mouth twisted up into the first hints of a smile Rockson had seen since he came in. "Once we analyze the sequences of words in *our* book, we can send it through the computer to re-do the edition Rahallah's using. That's the right track!" He immediately set the five cipher techs to figuring out just how to program the CC mainframe with the actual book before them. It took nearly three hours before they understood the right sequencing between words. But at last, success. Rock could see that Rath took a certain pride that his men were able to come through. And he congratulated him.

Once the message was completely unraveled, the linguistic experts turned over the sheet of paper with their scrawlings on it to the intel chief, who read it out, as Rockson listened intently:

"To rock son from your friend, the premier's aide, R. in Moscow: I think you and I trust one another. We've already been through battles together and you know my word is good. We face great danger. The madman kill love who we both believed to be dead is alive. I received a thought vision from my relative, a witch man from the Sudan. You will understand for you are a star pattern sensitive, capable of similar mental connections from time to time. His village was being destroyed by terrible weapons, by whole mountains falling. And I saw kill love's face in the midst of the bloodshed. Even as my uncle died in an instantaneous dissolution I

34

watched through his eyes, felt the final gasp, saw the skull's dark eyes coming toward the village.

I was able to use the premier's intelligence gathering services to find out what the skull is up to. It is perhaps the worst threat this planet has faced since the great war itself. He is conquering north Africa. Has already taken over large parts of Egypt. These terrible falling mountain weapons enabled him to do it. I have not been able to discover thus far how they work, how many there are. I know that he's taken control of some Egyptian cult, worshippers of the ancient sun god. Kill love's weapon can lift whole mountains, carry them along for hundreds of yards above the ground, and then drop them down on any target. He clearly plans to conquer and then use all of north Africa as his base of operations. He's moving very swiftly to consolidate power. He is clever. Even with these fearsome weapons, he needs a base of support. He needs a conquering army to follow behind his cult and take control. If my intelligence reports are accurate, he could control all of north Africa within another month. The entire continent within a few months. And then we both know he will not hesitate to move into Europe, Asia and then over to your country."

Rath, who was reading the message with a tremulous voice, paused for a moment as his eyes came up to meet those of Rockson, who could hardly believe his ears. Rockson knew, more than anyone, the depths of Killov's dark soul. And his ability, like some phoenix from hell, to climb out of the ashes again and again and resume his attempts at world conquest. Only he had never had as terrible a weapon as the one that Rahallah, the Soviet Premier's aide, spoke of.

Rath read on, after wiping his brow:

Rock son, you can imagine how I have tried to
get the premier to commit troops to combat this
threat. But the idea that the madman kill love
with an army of a few thousand sun worshippers could actually threaten the Soviet empire is
beyond his comprehension. The premier scoffs
at the very idea, making only vague promises to
send some elite soldiers down there. There are
riots throughout Russia; many cities are under
martial law. His attention is diverted elsewhere.
There will be no resistance from the Red Army
to the skull's designs until it's too late.

Which means, rock son, that by the time you
receive this, I will have already flown to Egypt to
try to help stop it myself. I owe it to the planet
earth itself to try, even if I am destroyed. I owe it
to my uncle and his people, who were wiped out
like so many ants beneath a boot. They are of
my blood. There was no one I was closer to.

I need aid. I need a man like you, rock son.
You have been able to defeat the skull before,
and send him packing. You have driven him
from power in your land. I know this is an incredible request on my part. You have many
problems and battles of your own going on at
this very moment. But I pray that you, above all
men, will understand the threat. I throw all
pride to the wind and beg you to come.

If you do, the following locations are where
I or my agents will meet you. I will wait two
weeks from the sending of this message. We will
come and check out the rendezvous point every
day. Then I and my fighters will be forced to begin the war against kill love on our own. I know

that many of your own people will think this is a trap. By the blood of the plains lion who is my namesake, by the blood of my uncle which was spilled, I speak true. May the spirits give you guidance. Please help.

Rath let the several pages of notes fall loosely in his hand as he stopped reading. He looked up at Rockson, and with as dark an expression as the Doomsday Warrior had ever seen the frozen face possess, he said, "It's a trap, Rockson. Killov's dead, we know that. The Reds are just carrying out all this elaborate bull to get your ass in tow and kick it down into the dirt!"

But Rockson looked the intel chief squarely in the eyes and said with absolute firmness, "I'm going, Rath. Not all the Council edicts in CC could stop me."

CHAPTER FIVE

There was a breakdown in four of the five power stations just when Rock called a meeting of his elite team. But that was hardly unusual around Century City. Things were continually breaking down. It wasn't that the men who made the underground city's machinery and equipment weren't skilled, but rather that they used poor materials—half the time leftovers from a century before. Their materials had been used, reused, and then used again, and were reaching the very limits of their durability. Even steel atoms had their breaking point!

But the "Rock Team" met by torchlight in one of the smaller conference rooms, three flashlights set upright on the table casting their faces into demonic-looking presences. McCaughlin, the joker of the group, was none too slow in commenting upon how "handsome" Archer appeared, or the fact that Detroit amost disappeared in the shadows with his midnight black skin.

"Can it," Rock said. Then Rock looked around the table at the men who had worked and fought and bled alongside him for years. Men who would walk anywhere beside him, fight any enemy—the devil himself, if Rockson asked them. Aside from his fighting prowess and mutant sixth sense which had saved them all more times than they liked to think about, Rock had something else—the ability to lead men. The ability to make them feel that he was going to get them through it all no matter what. And if somehow he didn't, well, not a one of them could think of a man they'd rather go down fighting next to than Rock.

He had already gone through in his mind just who to bring along for the cross-oceanic journey. They were all good-spirited, tough men, each a specialist in his own way, each with his own niche. Detroit, the black bull of a man, was shorter than Rock, but with shoulders and a chest that would have made Mike Tyson, the great heavyweight boxer of the last century, green with envy. Next to him sat McCaughlin, the huge Scotsman, cook, joke-teller, and general all-around bone-crusher when the going got rough. Then Chen, whose martial-arts abilities and exploding star knives made him, in Rock's mind, one of the toughest dudes on the face of the planet. Though they had sparred numerous times—sometimes one, sometimes the other coming out on top—Rock didn't look forward to ever really fighting it out with him. It was one battle he couldn't even imagine the outcome of. Then Archer, the towering seven-foot-plus near-mute who Rock had rescued from a quicksand pit years before. The man had been like an obedient puppy to Rock ever after, ready to dive into a volcano if Rock requested it. His tremendous strength and immense crossbow—which he carried around his back—made him a super combat man. Then Sheransky, the newest member of the Rock Team, a Russian defector whom the others had at first been very wary of, both because of his

Russian background and because they hadn't been all that happy about welcoming another man to their elite group. But after a few skirmishes with him along, after they had seen that the man was neither a traitor or a coward, but the equal in heart and ability of any of them, he had been warmly accepted.

Pound for pound Rock knew he was looking at the baddest bunch of asskickers around. And he also knew he could only take three of them with him on a trip from which they very possibly might not come back. Not with Killov holding the reins on a herd of mountains which he could raise up and squash down on you like you were a goddamned ant. So it made it hard to choose, both because they were most likely going to rejoin those dark ashes from which they had sprung—and because he knew his men would all want to be included in the fun and games more than anything on this earth.

But he had already made the decision. The choice could only be dictated by need, as logically and with as much foresight as possible. Rock had mulled it over in his "conventional" mind and then turned to his mutant sixth sense to see if the choices matched. They did. That made him feel certain of the correctness of it. For it meant that the left and right sides of his brain, and mutant factor, were working more and more in synchronicity these days. If he could ever get the whole damned nervous system operating at maximum, he'd *never* make mistakes!

Dr. Schecter was always urging him to push it, see what his mutant abilities really were, how far they extended. As if Rockson could somehow just snap his fingers and make it all happen. It wasn't that easy at all. But it was true. He could feel it, see the super abilities that lay just beyond him, tantalizingly out of reach. Abilities that were awesome compared to his

40

normal abilities. It was like this thing called enlightenment, from what he'd read about it. It was there—right in front of you, waiting for you to pick it up like an oyster from its shell. Yeah, right!

He suddenly spat out the names like bullets issuing forth from his mouth. "Chen, Archer, Sheransky—we're going to Africa. Maybe see some elephants." He smirked. "Tarzan too."

"Hey, Rock, now that ain't fair," McCaughlin said quickly. But Detroit was right behind him in his protests. None of the men could imagine that a Rock combat team would be quite complete without their specialized skills.

"Sorry, boys," Rockson replied, raising his hands. "I can only take three men, since most likely we'll be riding the skylanes in a Red MIG 7X fighter. It's a four-man job. Mostly because that's the only intercontinental jet I've had any real experience flying. Also, that's the main trans-oceanic jet of the Soviet occupation force. And since things have been quiet, they leave them lying around like transport trucks. I hear they're just parked along the edges of Red Air Force bases—with the keys hanging in them."

The men laughed.

"But that means four—that's all it seats. I've carefully gone over the most likely requirements for this operation. It's nothing personal. And besides, you two men will be CC's field operations commanders while I'm away. You're in line behind me for all military operations other than strictly defensive army operations of Century City. It's a necessity. I need you both here. We can't leave this place without some kind of real combat brains. Men who've really fought, who've bled, who know what the hell it's all about. Not just these aging generals who sit

41

around in their overly large offices twenty levels below the ground, plotting war games on half-busted computers."

The men laughed again. Rock had a way with words when he was in the mood.

The two men who were to be left behind—Detroit and the bear-sized McCaughlin—both brightened considerably at the words of praise. There was a lot of prestige attached to the field operations position, even if it was momentary. It would up their lot in CC at a number of different levels, not the least of which would be with those of the female persuasion. Perhaps most of all, the fact that Rockson trusted them—not just their battle prowess, but their intelligence and leadership abilities as well—made staying behind palatable. It was the greatest trust he'd ever placed in them.

"Anyway, that's the story, fellows—and we're leaving at dawn. I'm having some 'brids supplied up, though we're going to travel pretty light. Needless to say, we won't be taking the hybrid horses on the jet to Africa with us. Whatever we need we'll get there—in Africa, I hope. So sleep, eat, screw, whatever . . . but be ready and at the outer 'brid chamber at the stroke of six." Rock looked around at the men. "Any questions, comments, or problems with what I just said?"

Archer was squirming around in his seat like he had the question of the ages to ask, and Rock nodded toward the big man.

"Yeah." He grinned over the huge bushy beard with food particles from the last meal wedged firmly in numerous nooks and crannies. "I drink too much beer. If meeting over, I need *battthrooooommm*."

The whole room broke up, and Rock hooked his thumb toward the door.

"You understand—six o'clock—we go to Africa," Rock said. The towering Archer nodded vigorously. Rockson never quite knew for sure if the big fellow really knew what the hell he was talking about. Or if he just nodded yes with a crazed look in his eye because he had learned that was what Rockson wanted to see. Archer rose from the table and shot out the door like a rocket.

"Detroit, McCaughlin, come with me to my 'office.' I want to go over some of the things involved in combat ops." Rockson's office was a notorious and sick joke as far as he was concerned, a room hardly larger than a closet that the bunch of them could barely fit into at the same time. One dangling light bulb which sputtered as if it were thinking about supernova'ing out, a file which leaned at a steeper angle than the tower of Pisa and had botched requisition forms sticking out of it everywhere, and a desk.

"Look, I'm not going to go over all this bull that's in here," Rock said as he, McCaughlin, and Detroit stood inside the room. He pointed to the exploding files. "I've never looked at a word in there. The main thing is, should there be any need for field operations, you have to notify General Abrams or General Harris immediately. They're in charge of getting the units together, because if it's any kind of major attack that you have to launch—like a big Red convoy—we could be talking about other Freecities too, or at least thousands of men. You know the story. You've both been involved in full-scale military operations. Now, of course the generals will be in charge of the actual movements of troops, but they'll work with you. What it all means is that your roles would be to conduct a knowledgeable oversight for the whole mobile strike force. You make the decisions together,

43

and I mean that. You both know when and where the shit will hit the fan. They don't. Work around the generals if need be. I'll back both of you on this one hundred percent."

He looked them both hard in the eyes, back and forth, and then spoke more softly. "And God help you both should you need to buck the generals. Because it's always scared the hell out of me. It's not a responsibility that one carries easily. Now, I gotta get out of here. Got a date with a lady who'll kick my butt if I'm late." He winked and headed out of the room, leaving the two men to stare around in sudden horror at the overstuffed file, with the realization that they ran the "Field Operations" office now.

Rock stopped off at the hybrid horse stables on Level 2. The 'brids were just below the top level, so they could be gotten out of the city quickly in case of emergency. He found McKinley, the tall, still-acne-faced young man in his early twenties who ran the stables. He was exceptionally good with the animals. Rock had noticed that before. Rock came to the riding ring, where the lad was trying to train a wild 'brid that had been captured recently, and saw that McKinley had the extremely wild beast from the wastelands already turning in circles. The new 'brid was following the lad's basic instructions and tugs on the long training reins. The young man knew the secret of working with animals—make them want to please you. You never had to say a harsh word, or even hit the beasts. McKinley clearly knew that particular animal-truth, even if some other humans might not. The lad noticed Rock.

"I'm going to need full combat junk for three of your biggest and fastest 'brids," Rock yelled over to him. "I know Snorter has been having hoof problems," Rockson said, referring to the hybrid

44

horse that he had used for several years, an immense beast with more brains than a lot of humans he'd known. "So you pick someone good for me, okay? Need 'em by six A.M."

"Sure, Rock." McKinley smiled back. Even though he had seen the Doomsday Warrior walking around CC for years, and had helped to outfit a dozen or more of his other outings already, the young horseman still felt somewhat in awe of the man. "Full combat! Right!" McKinley beamed. "I'll pick the cream—the ones the generals like to use to parade around at parade time." The young horseman added with a wink, "We'll give them generals some mules!"

They both laughed, and Rock knew the guy was a winner. Maybe someday he'd invite him to take on a mission with the Rock team. On second thought, forget that, Rockson admonished himself. Century City needed a good horse-trainer far more than it needed another combat soldier, more fodder for the cannons.

"Oh, and I think Dr. Shecter's field-test boys will be bringing you a few new inventions for us to try out," Rock added. Shecter was a madman with his feverish attempts to constantly upgrade combat equipment. In a way, every time Rock and his men went out on a mission they were guinea pigs for all kinds of bizarre new Shecter-gear. Some of it had worked extremely well, had even saved Rockson's ass several times. Other inventions had been complete fizzles. "I told him to keep it under five pounds a man—and compact. So you shouldn't have too much trouble making room for it."

"Will do, Rock. I'll watch out for you, you don't have to worry about that none," McKinley replied. "I'll pack 'em right!"

"I ain't worrying, man," Rock said. "I got other

45

things to worry about." Rockson looked down at his watch—7:30. Rona was going to kick his butt all the way to Level 20 if he didn't move fast. Nothing makes a woman angrier than being stood up for dinner. Rockson had discovered that years before. But even though he took the back stairs three at a time, it still took him nearly ten minutes to get to the damned place. To make it properly romantic, the Sky Lounge was built at the top of the mountain in what was essentially a cave. When the elevators had worked, the club/lounge, built from faded woods and Art Deco antiques that search teams had found over the years, had been endearing. But now, with hundreds of feet of twisting metal stairs to climb, its charm seemed quite lost on Rockson.

He reached the lounge at last and barreled out through the emergency exit doors onto the long restaurant floor with its hand-carved stone tables set here and there among ivied pillars of marble. Above, the sky could be seen, though it wasn't actually right overhead. By cleverly rigging up a series of mirrors along a chasm that rose another hundred feet to the actual surface of Carson Mountain, the builders of the restaurant had created the illusion of the whole cosmos floating by overhead, day or night. From outside, no passing Russian spy drone could see it on video camera. The place was usually quite popular, being the only sector of the entire city that you could actually "see" the sky from. And though hunting and combat groups often went out into the "real" world, many others found themselves inside Century City for many months at a time. A trip to the Sky Lounge was essential for sheer mental health every once in a while, so they said. But not now!

"Where the hell have you been, mister?" Rona hissed, with icebergs in her voice. "Some damned meeting or other, I imagine. Perhaps you had to discuss with the council whether the triggers on the new automatic Liberator rifles should be two inches long or three?"

"Sorry, baby," Rockson said gently, leaning over as he approached her and kissing her soft and lightly perfumed cheek. "Ah, you smell mahv—ee—lous." He grinned his most charming grin as he plopped down in the seat next to her and looked down at his plate. His smile dropped, for the entire meal was already sitting there, and it looked quite cold and dead, and not very appetizing. Three-eared rabbit is tasty when hot and covered in a steaming cheese sauce, but this one—cold and coated with something orange and hard, with a few loudly buzzing flies already circling around its crevices—made him gulp hard. He pushed the plate away a few inches, not being able to quite look directly at it.

"Well, that's what you get for being late," she said. "I couldn't wait, see?" She pointed down to her plate, which was completely empty but for a single synthobean which dangled precariously at the end of the slightly chipped chinawear. "And it was delicious."

"I guess I screwed up, didn't I?" Rock said, raising his eyeballs as he confessed his guilt. Suddenly his stomach, which had finally gotten the message from his eyes that there was food sitting somewhere out there, began growling and telling him that it didn't care if the meal was living or dead, hot or cold—just that he'd better start eating right away or he was in trouble. It growled a few more times, and then gnawed at him with a horrible empty feeling as digestive acids already began dripping deep inside. Rockson reached slowly out with knife and fork and cut a piece of the gamey rabbit. The first bite was

47

hard to swallow. But by the third forkful he was actually enjoying it. "Better than trail food!"

She frowned.

After dinner, and a decent dessert of soycurd blueapple pie and then a drink or two, both he and Rona were felling pretty good, his lateness and cold rabbit long forgotten. In fact, with hardly anyone else there that night (too lazy or tired to make the long climb), it was quite romantic. The stars filled the wide curved, domed ceiling above as violinists played soft lilting music from a grotto off to the side. Rockson bowed to her and took her out on the dance floor, and they moved gracefully around, dancing in ever wider circles as they began moving faster. The few, mostly elderly, couples who were dining in the restaurant stopped their alimentary processes and watched the beautiful couple. They were a perfect match in a way, Rockson with his body chiseled down to stone and steel, and Rona, a dancer, gymnast, and seductress, with her flame-red hair swirling around her. It made even the oldest ones in the sparse audience sigh, and remember with bittersweet recollection their younger days.

Later, back in her bedroom—for his was far too small and cluttered—they made passionate love through the night, as she clung to him like a python around a tree, never wanting to let go.

CHAPTER SIX

Leaving her was the hard part. It always was. Rona's warm body clung to him in the darkness of the room as the wall clock whirred away with green hands inexorably turning. She felt and smelled like paradise itself, with her hot woman's perfumes and soft mouth constantly pecking at his neck and shoulders. He had to be a madman to give up this dream of sensuality and go into the murderous wastelands. But he lived for more than his own life. He lived to free his people, his country. He was a Freefighter.

So Rockson rose, made himself rise. And dressed, even as he heard her sobbing softly, not wanting to show him her tears. He leaned over when he was fully clothed and kissed her hard, and then turned and walked out of the room. He didn't hear the sobs turn to bawls the moment the steel door slid closed behind him.

The others were already there, standing alongside their fully packed 'brids, talking about the upcoming mission. That is, Chen and Sheransky were talking. Archer just grunted unintelligible noises from time to time, but seemed to be enjoying the conversation as much as the others. Rock was pleased to note they were fifteen minutes ahead of time. He didn't know they'd in fact all been there for an hour, each wanting to be the first.

"We're all battle-geared," Chen said as he stood next to his chestnut 'brid. "This fellow McKinley here is something else. We all went over our stuff on checklist, not missing a thing." The horse man, who stood off to the side making sure there were no last-minute problems, grinned with pride and looked down at the sawdust-covered stone floor of the outer cavern.

Rockson walked over to the 'brid that was his and came up to it slowly from the front so it could see him clearly.

"Name's Secretariat," the horse-handler shouted over from a loading platform where he stood leaning against a steel pole. "Named after one of the greatest twentieth-century racing horses. And I'll tell you what—this boy here could give 'em all a run for their money. He's just about the fastest 'brid we've got here. Probably ain't even been clocked at his best speed."

"Good boy, Secretariat," Rockson said as he reached out and patted its nose. He held out a handful of syntho M&M's, and the horse lapped them up like vitamins. Then it whinnied and raised its head, and Rockson saw that it was a strong, proud animal, high at the shoulders and with still-wild eyes. Eyes that told him it could run when it had to, and wouldn't bolt if it spotted a snarwolf or something worse.

"You've got a friend for life," Sheransky said, laughing. "Should have thought of it myself. This one keeps snapping at me." As if hearing his complaint, the 'brid kicked out a back foot that missed the Russian Freefighter by an inch.

"I want to get out there, hit some of the woods before the sun gets up high," Rock said as he walked to the side of his mount and leaped up onto the plastisynth saddle. "So take your final trip to the bathroom—and Archer, that means you—cause I don't want to stop until sundown."

Usually Freefighters out in the wastelands did just the opposite, moved at night when the Red drones couldn't see them as clearly, and rested in the day. But the direction they were heading in to "liberate" a Russian jet was hazardous, Rockson knew. The way was filled with earthquake chasms and steep and gravelly slopes. Traveling at night would be impossible. They wouldn't get a hundred yards in the night without someone getting hurt. They'd have to take their chances in the light.

"Open them up," Rock shouted across to the two guards with SMGs around their shoulders who stood on each side of the wide steel doors built into the side of the mountain. This was just one of a dozen such exits hidden around the base of the mountain, though this one was the largest as it was the main hybrid egress. The guards pulled at a large lever and the thing began chugging away, pulling the doors to each side. The dawn light filled a tunnel ahead that ran for about fifty feet. It was camouflaged, made to look like a bat-and-slime-encrusted cave. He soon reached the weed-and-leaf-woven camouflage netting. Rock slowed his 'brid and swept the netting aside in the middle with his arm so the creature could get his head through. It was all pretty crude, but from even a few yards away it looked pretty good.

They rode into the dawn, as the radioactive skies brightened by the minute. Far above, the undulating magnetic lines of purple and green ringed the earth,

51

filled with high radiation death, fallout from the twentieth century still releasing its poisons in flakes, rays, and God knew what all. The Northern Lights atomic-style. And yet it was beautiful as well. A radioactive rainbow in the dawn. Beauty was in the eye of the beholder, that was for damned sure. And if this was his world, then Rockson was sure as hell going to have to take beauty where he found it. Whether it be in the pearl-lustered shell of a snapping roach, or the oddly twisted black horns of the unicorn rams that were replacing normal mountain rams in the Rockies as the years went on. Rock was a mutant human himself. Who was he to judge the worth of other creatures? Whatever God gave them—that was their existence. For better, for worse, in ugliness, and in grandeur.

But such aesthetic thoughts passed quickly as the dawn sun rose higher, pulling its red face up into the sky like some bloated drunk who had slept one off in the gutter.

It was going to be a scorcher, Rock could see that after just an hour of riding. The sky, which was generally filled with odd-colored clouds or rings of one thing or another high above, things which often blocked out many of the direct rays of old Sol, had today decided to be perfectly clear. As the sun rose higher over the fir trees that surrounded them on the Rocky Mountains slopes, the sky above turned a crystal blue, the blue of expensive chandeliers in Soviet palaces.

The sun beat down on them like a searchlight searing at them with its gamma and ultraviolet and X-rays. Rock had them stop when he started feeling funny himself. No man, not even a mutant, could take the full, unfiltered rays of a twenty-first century crystal-sun. But Dr. Shecter had provided for this several years before, with one of his devices that really did work.

"Take out the reflector blankets," Rock said, reaching around his back. The packs that were tied around the rear of the saddles and over the broad back of the 'brids had been worked out years before with Rock's assistance. He and the other men knew just where to reach for their gear. Within seconds they held what looked basically like thick pieces of aluminum foil, and were unfolding them. Based on the "Space Blankets" of the twentieth century, these were the advanced models, virtually unrippable and capable of reflecting back nearly ninety percent of the sun's rays and heat. Within a minute they were all draped with the things, looking like foil-wrapped potatoes ready to pop into the oven. Chen's, Rock's, and Sheransky's fit fine. Archer had a special reflector—two of them glued together. And even then he was barely able to get it around himself, and to snap the velcro seals closed. It would have to do.

It was always somewhat slow going the first few hours out on any mission. It didn't make sense to push it. The men's bodies, the 'brids, everything had to fall into the right rhythm. Rock knew it would happen, and he let the animals get used to being out, let them find their own natural gait. The first few hours were hard anyway because of the steep slopes of the age-old Rocky Mountains. They rode up and down through forests of firs, across hillsides of wild purple and orange and blue mountain flowers bursting with fragrance so that they were almost covered with hordes of bees searching for early morning nectar. It was, in spite of the searing sun, an awesomely beautiful day. The men could see for miles when they reached the summit of each high hill, the Rockies stretching off in every direction as if

53

they covered the entire earth.

They traveled half the day, not even stopping to eat. Rock's men knew he wasn't one to stop for a pleasant little picnic. They ate on the move, throwing feedbags down over the 'brid's faces as the animals were capable of eating and moving at the same time. High in the saddle, the Freefighters took out their own concentrated energy packets and chugged from water jugs.

Still and all, they made fairly good time over the course of the day. By the time the sun was starting its slow descent to the west, like a kite that had run out of wind, they were already into some of the lower foothills. The southeast route they were taking was one Rock hadn't been on for years. It was a route that headed straight for the nearest Russian airport, some hundred and fifty miles away. Compasses were virtually worthless in this neck of the woods because of strong rad-deflected magnetic fields. But the mapping teams of Century City were always out and bringing back updated information. Every hour or so Rock took out the plastipaper map that showed the five hundred miles east and south of CC, checking on a particular mountain or some granite outcropping.

So far they were dead on target. He wanted to get up to a certain mountain pass before the sun completely dropped from sight, because it would mean easier travel the next day. According to the maps it was much smoother going on the far side. None of the men complained, though their butts felt like they were being ground down into what could have been sold for leather pocketbooks, if there had been such things anymore. Getting into the saddle always took a certain amount of readjustment, even for those who had been out numerous times before—like Chen and Archer. Sheransky had only had a few missions thus far, and he groaned and spat out soft little curses in Russian as the 'brid bounced up and down beneath him. But he didn't say a word to the others.

They reached the mountain pass just as purple-pated Sol disappeared behind a far glacial mountain. Rock hesitated as they reached the start of a valley about a mile long. It looked a little treacherous because of the gravelly ground, but the 'brids' hooves were as hard as steel. He made a decision and headed in. He was just starting to relax a little, after they'd gotten about halfway through the pass, when the shit hit the fan.

Actually it was bats that hit the fan of the rapidly darkening night air. It was as if they came out on cue the moment the sun fell completely behind the mountain, brought out by the darkness or the sudden cooling that hit once the warming sun had vanished. Whatever their reasons, the bats came out of small caves on each side of the mountain pass, by the thousands, by the tens of thousands. The flapping creatures flew out of their caverns like an army of leathery birds, and soared out with high-pitched squeals. The wrong kind of squeals for happy bats. These were blood-bats!

"Shit," Rockson barely had time to mutter as he saw the hordes come shooting out. As a bunch of the ugly little faces came barreling straight at him, he saw as well that they weren't the insect-eating variety. They were after something far meatier—men and hybrids. They weren't large, that was one thing anyway. So even as the first few scouts snapped down at him, Rock was able to brush them off, waving his hands wildly in front of him. The Freefighters all still had on the Shecter blankets, which gave them a certain amount of protection and seemed to confuse the bats. But the teeth of the blood-drinkers snapped closed over the outerwear over and over, trying to break through trying to get to the good stuff inside.

They were ugly, hideously ugly, Rock saw as he caught one in his hand, squeezed hard, and threw it off dead to the ground. They were more like flying teeth than the insect-eating bats he had seen in the past. Definite mutations, with fangs a good two inches long and slime-coated black bodies with spiderwebs of red veins throbbing all over their surface.

"Get the hell out of here, boy," he screamed into the 'brid's ear, kicking it hard in the flanks as it reeled around from side to side unsure where to go. But it let Rockson take over control, and the steed tore ahead as he loosened the reins. The other three hybrids followed quickly behind. The men were all shouting and waving their hands as the bats grew more organized and began making diving raids in groups of hundreds at a time. Some of them managed to snap their jaws shut right on the 'brids' sides or flanks, searching for blood. As the steeds galloped along terrified, bellowing out whinnying sounds of sheer terror, a number of the blood-drinking bats managed to attach to their sides, flopping around from the motion of the animals. But they hung on as their teeth drew out the red liquid from beneath the thick outer hides like syringes.

As the cloud of twisting and turning bat-bodies grew ever thicker, Rock pulled out his shotpistol and aimed it straight ahead, where a huge group of the things seemed to have turned and were coming straight at him in a squadron, as if trying to stop the whole caravan so they could feast fully. Rock pumped the shotpistol and blew dozens of them away—and on the second shot dozens more. Behind him he heard more gunshots, and then saw some of Chen's shuriken starknives whizzing up into the air, taking out large groups as they exploded.

Masses of bloody fangs and broken wings flew around like wet shrapnel. But even as the blood-bats fell to the gravel-strewn ground of the mountain pass by the thousands, more came in. There were just too many. There was no way to fight them.

Rock felt two of them land on the base of his neck at the same time, one on each side, and had to tighten his legs around the saddle. He reached up with both hands and ripped the things free, squeezing as hard as he could, like a man bending a Bud after drinking it down. He could hear the bones crunch and the sharp squeals of the things as he tightened and then threw them to the dirt. He could feel the blood oozing down his neck as well. The little bastards had managed to break the skin. He prayed they didn't inject a poison. But the 'brids still were galloping faster than ever and doubtless some of the first bites would have affected them by now if the bats were poisonous.

Still, as he fired the last of his shots and reached for another quick load, Rock could see they weren't making a dent in the attacking waves. Somehow he wouldn't have minded dying fighting Reds, or helping Rahallah battle Colonel Killov. But to go out here, on their first night of the mission, consumed by these ugly little dudes—please God let it not be so. He glanced up quickly at the darkening sky as if someone might be up there listening. And there was. But it wasn't the Big Guy.

And even as his eyes came down again, there was a fiery roar about fifty feet ahead of him and perhaps twenty feet up, right where an approaching flock was

57

the thickest. Flames shot out in every direction and Rockson was totally confused for a moment, even as he watched thousands of the blood-bats burst into flame and drop from the sky like burning leaves from a forest fire, the fiery wings etching crazy patterns in the dusk. Then another mini-explosion, and another, and bats were dropping like moths that had strayed too close to the flame.

Rock suddenly realized that it wasn't lighting bolts from the blue—but Archer. They were arrows from his crossbow, tipped with phosphorous bombs, just one of many ingenious arrowheads that the huge Freefighter—with Shecter's lab boys' help—had rigged up. He turned in his saddle and saw the Freefighter fitting arrow after arrow into the groove of the thing, pulling them from the quick-fire quiver he had strapped beneath the crossbow. With its instant spring-controlled reload, he could shoot the arrows out every second or two. And he was doing so with a vengeance.

Bats fell like flies. And as more and more of the flaming arrows flew and burst through the curtains of the flying blood-drinking mammal, the bonfire of wings and teeth grew. Rock saw that the blood-bats were actually setting each other on fire as well. Wings touched other wings as they soared down from the air in pain-maddened squealing circles. And others hesitated to join the fiery party.

Suddenly the flock was too concerned with survival to worry about food and they pulled back, an immense cloud of them veering off away from the attack as they saw their blood-drinking comrades turned into overdone Bat-B-Q on the ground below. Rock didn't slow down an inch, kicking his 'brid hard, not that the animal needed much prodding. And then they were through it, out of the pass and barreling down into a meadow of purple flowers, their heads bent over like monks in prayer as the night air fell. They didn't stop for nearly ten minutes and when they did, both men and 'brids were breathing hard, eyes wild. It had been a few terrifying minutes none of them would ever forget.

As the Freefighters dismounted to give the heaving 'brids a chance to rest, and to quiet their own pounding hearts, Rock slapped Archer hard on the back. As the near-mute took the congrats of Rockson and the other fighters, a big smile etched across his broad-bearded face. He was so happy that he could contribute to the team. Rockson looked at Chen and Sheransky and spoke with a sigh as soft as the breezes that wafted up the mountain slopes. "Thank God the blood-bats are flammable."

"This" bunch is flammable," Chen said, "but how about the next?"

CHAPTER SEVEN

Once Rockson was absolutely, positively, one-hundred-percent sure that no more of the bat-things were after them, he holstered his shotpistol. They had torn ass for a good three miles in the near darkness lit only by the swirling strontium clouds high above and the pinpoints of starlight that stabbed through here and there. Rock hoped they were someplace safe—and on the charts—but there were things to do first before checking on that. Rockson inspected his mount, and the others did as well. There were a few bats still hanging on to Sheransky's and Chen's hybrids, but they were pulled off and disposed of with knives and under boots. The men made faces as they dealt with the bloodsuckers. There was just something about mankind and bathood that never did and never would get along. Their demonic overtoothed faces didn't help matters any. Underneath the 'brids, on their stomachs and flanks, their riders found numerous little bite marks still oozing traces of blood. None of them looked life-threatening, but they sure as hell had to be treated. You didn't go around oozing the red stuff in post-nuke America and expect to live very long. There were numerous carnivorous creatures out in those woods which would leap out at the very scent of blood. And most of them made the blood-bats look like mosquitoes.

So the Freefighters took antibiotic salve out of their med packs and slopped it on over the little gouges, checking every square inch of the 'brids, even around their hoofs, behind their ears, and under their manes. In fact Rock found a small bat hiding in Secretariat's thick mane, and pulled it off with repulsion. Up close the little things were even more disgusting than from a few feet away. He broke its neck with a sharp crack of his hand, and threw it in a small bag so that he could take it back to Shecter. The mad doctor was happier than a kid with a new toy when exotic species were brought back from "the outside." Rockson had never seen this particular brand of mini-hell before, so he assumed Shecter hadn't either.

At last everything was salved, cleaned, and sealed up and they mounted the 'brids again. Rock debated whether they should pack it in for the night now, but figuring they were still close to the flying teeth, and admitting the fact that both men's and animals' heart rates were up to ramming speed from all the adrenaline that had been pumped inside their veins, he thought he might as well take advantage of it. They'd get a few more miles under their belt!

In fact, the sky started clearing nicely, as if apologizing for the nasty little incident before. The green strontium clouds far overhead diminished to mere wisps and the clear sky, a trillion stars, and a bright scythe moon gave them plenty of light over the meadows and fields.

So they rode on through a landscape disconcertingly peaceful, with only the sounds of hoot owls and an occasional howl of a snarwolf in the distance for musical accompaniment to the clip-clop of their steeds' steps. Rockson drove them until nearly midnight, and then found a piece of high ground which looked secure. They bivouacked, giving the 'brids all the chow and water they wanted. After doing the same for themselves, the humans—except for watchful Rockson—fell fast asleep, ready to awaken at the slightest disturbance. There were none, other than in their bloody dreams.

The morning sun broke like a sun of the old days, before the nuke war. There were birds chirping, sunbeams dancing, and mountain flowers waving energetically in the morning breezes. All of them awoke with smiles. Facing death and surviving can put a man in a good mood. And after some hydroponically grown coffee, why, they were feeling positively chipper. Camp was broken, the 'brids resaddled and bridled, and within twenty minutes of rising, they were off.

They made excellent time that whole day, hitting no real obstacles and not a single thing that tried to eat, claw, or mutilate them—other than some swarms of mosquitoes and black flies, which they rode through from time to time and which lingered for minutes and then headed off. They were basically in a barren no-man's-land for the next seventy miles or so—a place where no Freefighters lived, and the Reds rarely ventured. Rock was unable to relax even though he knew it was extremely unlikely that they'd run into any spy drones which might relay their images back to some basement Red headquarters and precipitate a whole shitload of choppers coming out after them. In the mountains and forests it was easy enough to hide. But out here in the open with no real cover for miles in any direction they would be sitting ducks. But nothing happened. Just another day's ride.

They bivouacked again for the night, just beneath a rocky overhang of a low hill, where they were virtually invisible from above. He let the others take sentry duties, splitting it up among themselves. He needed some Z's bad, as he had done a double shift the previous night. He fell off fast, as if tripping down a cliff, and didn't move an exhausted muscle for seven hours. When he awoke, the morning was overcast and the air smelled foul and dead, as if after a few days of nice weather the earth was going to spit up some of the poisons that man had shoveled down her throat. The other men were in foul tempers almost immediately upon awakening, their throats raw, eyes tearing from a sulphurous smell in the air. Even the 'brids, which generally didn't pay much attention to air pollutants, were acting sluggish and kept snorting as if trying to spit something up.

They rode through the gray day into increasingly arid terrain. Even though it was clouded up, they had to bring out the Shecter blankets again and drape themselves from the hot rays of the sun. They pulled their legs up onto their mounts and just sort of tranced out as the animals made their tired way one grinding step at a time through the prairie land. Far off to the north Rock saw several jagged atomic-crater walls on the horizon, looking like still-festering sores on the face of the Earth. When they at last saw another range of mountains in the distance, everyone's demeanor took a turn for the better. Even the hybrids poured on the gas, wanting to reach the green-treed shade and some water, to get away from the sour smell of the dry red dirt beneath their hooves.

Thus they reached the Blackface Mountains—so

named because of the almost shimmering black coating over their surfaces, the result of nearby bomb blasts. They were marked on Rock's map as "safe."

It was sundown, but he pushed them a little, making the strike force head up into the foothills. According to the map, the Red air force base of Mesdinsk was just over the rise. It was built on a long flat plateau nearly two miles long and a thousand feet or so wide. The 'brids didn't like the idea of not stopping to graze on the slopes, green as they were—not after tramping through the wasteland dirt which made their hooves burn as if acid had been poured on them, which made their legs tremble beneath their powerful bodies as if they might give way. But somehow they walked on. Slowly, reluctantly, they stomped one angry leg down and then another.

They reached the summit, a good seven hundred feet up at a forty-five degree angle. Rockson had them all slow down before they got to the very top. The silhouette of a man on 'brid could be seen for miles there. Not that the Reds would be expecting anyone to be coming in from this direction. Most of the fortress cities and outpost bases weren't even that well guarded anyway. They were a lazy bunch, these bastards, Rock mused. After a century of occupation, the Russian troops had grown bored, fat, tired, like any entrenched bureaucracy. They had experienced few attacks on their main bases, as the Freefighters preferred to concentrate on convoys or on an occasional strike against a particularly important city. Some of the out-of-the-way bases, like the airport below them, almost coexisted with the small bands of Freefighters who often lived within miles of them. Just leave us alone—we'll leave you alone. For the moment anyway. Only the moment was now up.

The men dismounted from their steeds, tethering them to some stunted blue-barked trees just below the rise, and slid up on elbows and knees until they were looking down over the air force base. It was a long runway, designed to take intercontinental transport jets when necessary. But only a single runway ran along one side of the low barracks houses.

Rock took out his night-binocs and scanned the area. It was a typical Russian setup. They had designed the structure of these bases a century before, and that was that. No change in one hundred years. Which made it that much easier for anyone who had any designs on messing with them.

Eight MIGs were parked along a wide concrete corridor at one end of the two-mile-long runway, along with two of the MIG X7 four-seaters that Rock had prayed would be there. He let out a deep breath. So far so good. Two immense StratoBursters sat like steel whales side by side, so fuel supplies had clearly been delivered recently.

At the other end of the runway, set back about a hundred yards, were rows of two-story barracks, sealed off from the outside world like Howard Hughes's bedroom, so that not an American germ nor a particle of American radioactive debris could enter. About midway along the runway the control tower, a desultory globe-topped structure, rose up about sixty feet, high enough so controllers could direct air traffic, what there was of it, along the tarmac. It wasn't even lit up. They had clearly closed down for the night. Not a hell of a lot of call for air control after dark out here in the high-rad sticks of mutilated America!

Even for a Red base, the place looked pretty run-down. Rock knew the system. Only those bases, army command centers, etc., with high-ranking, well-connected officers got much of anything. There probably wasn't anybody above the rank of captain out here. So they had to deal with the crappiest equipment, food, and barracks.

Rockson almost felt sorry for the poor bastards who were holed up inside those little tin sardine cans, scared to even come out most of the time. Stuck there for years—often five, six, even as much as ten years—before they were allowed to return home. If they were still alive. They were hardly listed in the Moscow Who's Who out here. And if the whole damned base disappeared in some mega-storm or was sucked down in an earthquake, those back in the Kremlin weren't going to do a hell of a lot of mourning.

This base's very isolation—and the habits the air force officers had gotten into of closing the doors, pulling down the blinds, and waiting for the years to pass—was going to be very helpful to Rock and his team. He noted the two guard towers at each end of the place. These appeared to be manned. There were dim lights on inside the amber-tinted windows on the thirty-foot-high sentry boxes. They'd have to get those.

After he'd checked the place for a good five minutes, up and down, back and forth with his glass, trying to peer into every nook and cranny, he pulled back away from the rise as the others followed suit.

Archer was looking at him with huge brown eyes as he grunted out pitifully, *"FOOOOOODD? EEEEAAATT NOOOOWWW?"* The near-mute, just because of his immense bulk, was more like a grizzly than a man. He had to deposit uncountable pounds of chow into the large mouth each day in order not to starve. But tonight the oversized

Freefighter was going to have to make do with an energy pill.

"So now ve rest up and attack in the morning?" Sheransky asked hopefully, as he stretched tiredly, looking forward to a good night's sleep, to be rested up for their assault.

"No," Rock said, as his mind already was planning feverishly the best way to carry out the attack. "We're going in tonight. In fact, relieve your bladders, boys, 'cause we're moving right now. You might not get a chance to piss again all the way to Africa."

CHAPTER EIGHT

"A diversion. Somehow we've got to create something to divert the Reds' attention from our hijacking of the X7," Rock said as the men crouched down around him in the darkness, popping down a few super-energy and vitamin pills, a creation of the Bio boys back in CC. The pills didn't substitute for food, they didn't even take away the stomach's growling hunger, but they gave enough fuel in an emergency situation to keep a man going a good twelve hours without any energy loss. Sheransky popped his down in a depressed manner. Archer swallowed a whole handful of the things and eyed the feedbag around the 'brids heads with envy. Chen had his own concoction—super-hard crackers of Miso and God knew what Oriental energy concoction that he chewed on slowly instead of taking the bio pills. He sat in a crouch, almost invisible in the night air in his ninja suit, which cloaked him in a curtain of black against the other blackness.

"Some kind of dramatic happening down there," Rock whispered. "Even with those bastards watching their videos of rowing contests on the Volga and their sitcoms about masturbating tractors from

Mother Russia, someone's very possibly going to see something. We gotta wheel one of those X7 babies around, maybe even fuel her up—plus I'm going to need a few minutes at the controls to familiarize myself with how to fly the damn thing. It's been a while."

The last few words didn't exactly make them all feel any better. Sheransky gulped hard and downed another energy chunk. But they didn't say a word. It was a given from the start that when on a mission with Rockson, life could be terminated at any second. Still, they prayed he at least had some vague ideas about the functioning of the super-jet.

"All right then, this is the plan," Rockson said as he finished gulping down a few of the bio pills himself with a big slurp of water. "Sheransky, you'll come with me. If there's anyone around the jet parking lot, maybe we can fake our way in. You're a real Russian, and therefore have a much better accent than mine. That might get us in without firing. Archer, Chen, you two will go to the far end of the runway and wait for trouble. If you hear nothing, just wait. We'll come pick you up at that end. If you do hear or see trouble up where we are, set that far sentry post on fire. That'll draw them all to that end. Once you've got their attention, circle back along the perimeter of the field—to the midway point— and we'll taxi there in the X7—and we're on our vacation cruise."

It all sounded simple enough. None of them had any illusions that it was going to even come close to being that way!

Rockson went over the plan again so everyone understood just what they were supposed to do. They synchronized combat watches. Chen and Archer would begin their penetration of the field at exactly

11:00, just as Rock with Sheransky, made his move to hijack one of the jets. They unloaded their gear from the 'brids' backs, took off the saddles and reins from the beasts, and sent them on their way back down the slope in the direction they had just come from. All of Century City's 'brids were trained to make their way home once their riders left them or were killed. Only about a third actually ever made it home from distances like this. But that was better than none. And those that did were considered the toughest of a tough breed. Good breeding stock. Maybe the ones that didn't make it back survived out in the wild, who knew?

"Good luck, boys," Rockson whispered into the darkness as the hybrids picked up speed, realizing they were on their own again and headed off fast into the hills beyond. Rock muttered an inaudible prayer that the Diety would take care of them. Then the men were off over the top of the rise, splitting up into two groups. Chen and Archer headed down the slope to the left, Rock and Sheransky to the right. Archer, for all his attempts, had just never quite gotten the crouch-and-run down right. He was just too big. It was like a bear trying to limbo. Funny and sad.

Rock had to go slower than he normally would as Sheransky, though he was in fairly good shape and had been working out like a maniac in the CC gym for months, wasn't near the physical conditioning of the other men on the team—let alone Rockson himself. Rock would have been a super-athlete in the twentieth century, with offers for endorsements for every soft drink, car, and charge card known to man, so he had to hold back a little. Rock kept a sharp eye on the field as they descended toward it, making sure no one spotted them. It took about five minutes to get down the steep loose-graveled slope, and then they

70

ran outside a fence, around the base, through gullies, and over mole holes the size of the tunnel Alice fell into Wonderland in. The Reds clearly weren't busting their humps to keep the perimeter in shipshape condition.

They were rounding the far end of the fence with the jets in sight sitting parked like metal behemoths of the night. Rock was just starting to think they were going to get inside without too much trouble when a jeep came out of nowhere, its searchlight suddenly snapping on and swinging around onto them.

"Shit," Rock hissed, "down, down." He knew Sheransky wasn't as combat hardened and that his reflexes were slower. And true to form, the Russian defector seemed confused for a moment, and suddenly took off to the right for some bushes, stumbling around like a jackrabbit with one leg. The two Reds in the jeep saw only the running Sheransky and somehow missed Rock, who had ducked down fast, a situation Rockson took instant advantage of. As the jeep veered wildly around toward the stumbling Sheransky, Rockson came tearing out of the darkness with his long knife blade in hand. He leaped with everything he possessed in his steel legs, and managed to get up onto the back of the jeep even as it continued its pursuit.

The guy who was sitting on back of the jeep, handling the light machine gun that was mounted there, didn't even see Rock. But he felt the cold steel, which sliced once deep across his neck. And he felt the blood shooting out of him in a waterfall. But only for a second. Then he was hurtling off the jeep into permanent darkness. The driver heard something at the last instant and reached for his service revolver. Rock jumped all the way to the front of the jeep with a leap, and slammed the knife down hard into the

71

Red's upper back. The blade penetrated muscle, bone, and the heart, slicing it in two like a badly butchered Sunday roast. Spurting blood from his mouth, the Russian didn't even have a chance to scream as Rockson kicked him from the driver's seat, taking over the wheel and bringing the vehicle to a stop.

Quickly he turned off the floodlights, leaving only the jeep's amber-colored low lights on in front.

"Pst, Sheransky," Rockson whispered into the darkness around the jeep. He heard rustling sounds and spoke up again sharply, just in case the Freefighter didn't realize that Rock had taken control of the jeep. Suddenly Sheransky came bolting out of the shadows, his silenced mini-Liberator submachine gun cradled in his hands like he was out for bear.

"All right, you Red bas—" the defector began. But he barely got two steps before he saw Rock and the gun lowered in his hands. "Oh, Rock, sorry, I thought—"

"Get in," the Doomsday Warrior snapped. "We don't have time to play around out here."

"Sure, Rock, sure." The blond Russian cursed himself silently. He was lucky Rock even took him on missions, he thought. Why the hell was he so slow sometimes? Rockson wheeled the jeep back around in the direction it had come from, and when he spotted the two dead guards lying about fifty feet apart, he stopped. He and Sheransky got out and donned their clothes, blood-splattered and torn as they were.

It was a pathetic disguise, Rock had no illusions about that, but he hoped that if they were seen it would be from a distance, in the darkness. It would have to do.

He started the jeep up again and headed it around the back end of the runway. As they came around the corner of the cyclone fence, he saw a gate about a hundred feet ahead and a single guard sitting back on a chair reading some well-thumbed Russian magazine under a flashlight. Probably porno.

"Sheransky, get your SMG ready—just in case. But I'm going to try to bullshit our way through. Tilt your head and mutter something dumb in Russian if the bastard looks up. If he looks up a second time, take his head off."

"Will do, Rock," Sheransky said, brightening a little after his fiasco of several minutes earlier. He cradled the SMG as Rockson came out of the darkness fast, cornering around through the opened gate. The guard glanced up quick, but fortunately for the two Freefighters, he had just reached the centerfold of his magazine. A centerfold containing an immense Russian woman with equally immense breasts. He stared down hard as the vehicle tore through, and Rock breathed out a sigh of relief. If they had been stopped before they even got inside, the firefight might have been too intense to get hold of the X7. Now at least they had a chance at it.

Rock tore right toward the aircraft-parking area. Most of the jets were completely unready for flight, the smaller ones chained down to protect them from the fierce winds that sometime swept across the land like a hurricane. Others had their wheels with blocks all around them. But two of the jets, one a MIG X7, stood side by side facing the long runway. Rock prayed the X7 was functional.

As they drew closer, he saw a grease-covered tech fiddling around with the wheels of the MIG. God was on their side tonight, maybe. Rock brought the jeep to a screeching stop, and was out and heading straight toward the man before he had a chance to realize what was going on.

The Russian tech began to rise from where he had been lying on his back looking up at the front wheel housing of the jet. He reached for his service revolver as he realized something was wrong, realized that the two men coming straight at him were not Piskov and Masilowski, the two night guards.

"Don't even think of it, comradeski," Rock snapped with a commanding tone as he aimed his shotpistol right at the tech's nose from about a foot away. The guy could get a good look at how big the barrel was, how it would take his head off with a single shot. Sheransky added a few choice threats in Russian as he also leveled his silenced SMG. The tech got the message, and let his hand fall away from the pistol as he rose up to full height with hands above his head. Rock reached down and took the revolver, slipping it into his belt. The mechanic was covered in grease and dirt, and looked more like a chimney sweep of Olde England than a technician who handled the most advanced aircraft in the world. But then Rockson was sure he and Sheransky were equally debonair in their blood-soaked Russian uniforms.

"Tell the dude that I want this X7 fueled up to the gills and everything ready to go—in ten minutes tops," Rock said to Sheransky, not wanting to waste the time with his poor Russian pronunciation. Sheransky snarled at the tech, spitting out a mouthful of Russian commands. The tech gulped hard several times and nodded his head vigorously in the affirmative.

"Says sure he'll do it," Sheransky said, turning to Rockson but keeping his SMG trained right on the man's heart. "But I'll keep a close eye on him. I don't trust how easily the bastard went along with it."

"What did you tell him?" Rockson asked as he glanced around a full three hundred and sixty degrees to see if anyone else was nearby. No one was. "You spoke too fast for me."

"Just said that we were bandit cannibals from the mountains." Sheransky smirked. "And that if he fucked with us, we'd cut out his heart for our dinner, and cut off his balls and send them back to Russia so his wife would see what she was never going to get again. The second part of the statement I think got to him." Rock winced at the thought, and jumped up onto the wing of the sleek jet, making his way along the inner edge up into the cockpit. Its long bubble dome was opened back. He sat down in the pilot's seat and looked at the controls with a groan. He had flown one of the jets about two years earlier, using a manual and praying real hard. Somehow he had pulled it off, but it sure as hell looked a lot more complicated tonight than it had then. He wondered if they'd changed the damned control panels.

He breathed out hard and began looking through the dog-eared flight manual which was sitting on the instrument console. He started fiddling with the various buttons and dials without actually pressing them in. Slowly it started coming back to him. But it looked like it was going to be more difficult than he had remembered, as some modifications had clearly been made to this MIG.

Suddenly there was a flash of bright light at the far end of the runway, followed by an explosion.

"Shit," Rock spat out. Chen and Archer had been discovered, or were creating a diversion too early. Whatever! Things were speeding up and they weren't anywhere near ready to take off.

"What the hell's happening down there?" Rock

screamed down at Sheransky as he saw troops running out of their barracks about a mile down the tarmac, heading toward the source of the explosion.

"Almost done, Rock," the Freefighter shouted back up again. "Dude says we're about three quarters full of fuel—another five minutes."

"Move it man, *move*," Rock screamed out again. "We may have to leave without a full tank if—" But he hadn't even gotten the words out when he saw a whole squad of Reds rushing down the asphalt toward the jets.

"Get in, man, forget it—we've got enough for the moment—we can refuel somehow, somewhere else—" Rock climbed half out of the cockpit, leaning over the side to see what the hell was taking so long. And even as he looked down he saw that as Sheransky climbed up the ladder propped against the side of the X7, the tech had grabbed a huge wrench and was just a mini-second away from bringing it down on the Freefighter's skull.

"Ah, shit," Rock groaned, ripping out his shot-pistol. He knew it was a matter of fractions of a second until Sheransky either lived or died. But his own mutant reflexes were slightly faster than the tech's, even starting with a handicap. Rockson's shotpistol rang out just as the mechanic began his descent toward the back of Sheransky's neck. The Russian Freefighter was still blissfully unaware of what was transpiring. He looked up to see Rock's huge-muzzled 12-gauge pellet-firing handgun aimed at what he thought was his head. He turned white as a ghost, wondering if somehow the Doomsday Warrior thought that he had betrayed them.

The gun went off with an explosion that made his ears do handstands. But the mechanic just inches behind him had worse problems. His whole face

76

disappeared into a grimy red mush that splattered out into the air as he fell backwards down onto the cement.

"In, *in*," Rock screamed out angrily as Sheransky froze for a few seconds on the ladder, even as the other guards began opening up with their weapons. The Russian Freefighter got the message that this wasn't the best place to be as a slug whistled past his ear and pinged off the ladder. He made it to the top of the cockpit, and Rock's strong arms reached out and grabbed hold of his sleeve, pulling him in so he slammed down onto the floor.

"Buckle in," Rock said pointing to the co-pilot's seat alongside his. There were two low-slung seats behind them for flight navigator and bombardier. Just enough room for Chen and Archer if they ever got to them. Which problem Rockson wasn't even worrying about right now as he bit his lip hard and threw the SYSTEMS ON switch. He was sure you were supposed to wait five minutes or so to actually fire up the plane after it was gassed up. Or so it said in the manual. So he waited ten seconds—and that was hard. But the jet, though it grumbled, the whole thing shaking wildly, fired up hard, a blast of red flame shooting out the back, along with some bolts and nuts.

He turned the half wheel sharply to the right and threw on some power. The MIG spun around, wheels screeching like some psychotic drag-racer's car on a back road. The funnel of exhaust flame poured right into the faces of several overzealous Reds, and they went up in flames, their hair, clothes, faces all burning brightly in the night. More shots rang out as Rock headed the jet out of the parking area and onto the runway. He heard a few more pings around the metal outer structure of the jet, but figured if it didn't blow up, he wasn't doing so bad.

Sheransky strapped himself in as he kept ducking down, hearing shots whistle by overhead since the cockpit's bulletproof dome was still in the open position. Rock had a few more passengers to pick up.

He guided the throbbing jet down the white-lined runway, the MIG jerking from side to side as Rockson tried to get the hang of it. Not that he had more than seconds. For even as they approached the far end he could see that Chen and Archer were in trouble. The Reds had set up mortars and heavy machine guns all around the two men. He could see them halfway up a small hill just the other side of the base fence. They hadn't even reached the fence! The Russians were opening up on the two of them like they were facing an army.

But Rock had his own equalizer now. And even as the jet moved to within a hundred yards of the air force troops, he opened up with a fusillade of its explosive machine-gun slugs. The bullets ripped through flesh and metal, fence and dirt, leaving bloody pools all along the side of the field. Two of the mortars and one machine gun stopped firing as they joined in the rain of smoking steel. Rock stood up, poking his head through the cockpit opening, and waved his hand up and down hard, signaling for the two trapped Freefighters to lie down flat where they were. They got the message, and stopped firing and flattened themselves out, though Archer's barrel butt poked up some from behind a boulder.

Rock sighted up through the computerized firing grid on the console, and then slammed his hand down on the firing button of the jet's air-to-air missile system. The jet shook like it was having a little fit, and then a missile shot out from under one

78

of the wings. At just a few hundred feet the explosion was quite loud, and the jet shook violently from the shock waves. But when the smoke cleared Rock saw that he had indeed made an instant access route through the airfield fence.

Archer and Chen came barreling out of the smoke and onto the runway as more of the Reds opened up again. The two men darted this way and that, Chen throwing out shuriken after shuriken from beneath his sleeves. The whirling five-pointed blades spun with a terrifying whistling sound through the air, ripping into whatever he had aimed them at—man or machine. They exploded with nearly the force of a grenade. And more of Lenin's men got to meet their Maker a little quicker than they had been expecting to.

Even as they rushed forward, Rockson again ripped the controls around, and the jet screeched around too, doing a 180 in about forty feet. He pulled the thruster back so the jet flame in the back went low but didn't die out, so the two Freefighters wouldn't be cooked to overdone before they even had a chance to get aboard. Then he heard cursing and scrambling, and even as he turned his head around, the two of them were somehow clambering up on board.

"Behind me," Rockson screamed out as they both tumbled inside, Archer almost landing on his lap and sprawling out onto the steel floor. He didn't wait to see if they were all tucked in nice and cozy, but pulled the thruster back to nearly half. The whole jet shook again, and they could smell the acrid odor of burning fuel as the exhaust flame lengthened to seventy feet spitting out behind them. They were pressed back into their seats by acceleration.

Just as Rock saw a Russian aim a bazooka-type

79

weapon from only about sixty yards dead ahead, he pulled the wheel towards his chest. The computer read-out indicated that they had enough thrust to get airborne. The canopy shut, the jet shot forward like a Brahma bull coming out of the rodeo gate, and slowly rose up. And they didn't even hear the piercing scream of the bazooka man as he melted like silly putty beneath the searing heat of the blast.

Why couldn't Rock get her higher?

The jet tore down along the runway at an altitude of ten feet as Russians came out from everywhere trying to strike down the intruder. More shots rang out—tracers, clouds of smoke as larger weapons went off. They were definitely ready to sacrifice the jet to get the suckers inside who had stolen it. Ahead Rock could see three armored vehicles tearing ass straight toward the slowly rising MIG from the far end of the tarmac, firing away with heavy machine guns.

"Hold onto your fucking hairpieces," Rock bellowed out above the roar of the overtaxed engine. He had just found the takeoff thrusters. "We're going up." He wasn't sure himself if he meant going up in the air or exploding—but he flicked the switches and pulled back hard on the control just as they reached the first of the advancing armored vehicles. The MIG took off straight up. Its right wheel slammed into the men who were shooting from the lead armored vehicle, sending them flying. The tail flames of the MIG ripped over the rest of the attacking vehicles, sending them all into flames as the three vehicles skidded wildly end over end, erupting in more fire as their gas tanks went up.

Somewhat to Rockson's disbelief the jet hit 2000 mph, the afterburners clicking in automatically to give him extra vertical boost.

They climbed up, rapidly losing sight of the bodies

and then the rooftops of the air base. Up over the smoke-filled air of the battle scene below they rose like a skyrocket on the Fourth of July. Sheransky let out a little cheer, and even Archer grunted up something congratulatory. A thin smile raced back and forth across Rockson's face. He was as amazed as the rest of them that they had pulled it off.

CHAPTER NINE

"Rock, Rock!" Sheransky screamed out as Rockson took the MIG X7 up in a steep climb, turning sharply so they all slid over at nearly a ninety-degree angle. Archer, who hadn't had time to strap his huge bulk in, was thrown from atop the seat and sent slamming into the steel frame of the canopy a few feet off. "They're sending up jets after us," the Russian Freefighter bellowed in his heavily accented English as he stared out the window nearly straight down at the miniscule moonlit runway below.

"Oh, are they?" Rock replied. He quickly banked the jet back around again so they all felt like they were going to fall out the other side. Archer, bellowing out slobbering curses, slammed all the way across the plane behind the second pair of seats, where Chen had managed to get himself belted in, and bashed himself into the other wall. Only his steel hide kept him from getting seriously hurt, but he was getting bruised up pretty good. His bearded face raked across the protruding ribs along the inside of the jet.

"Get strapped in, Archer. No heroics!"

Rockson leveled the plane out again, and they

could see that he had turned completely around so they were heading back toward the runway from about ten miles off. Rock could see the thrusters of three jets on the far end of the tarmac already firing up, red tongues of flame in the grayness below. He knew he probably wasn't good enough to take them all out in dogfights. That took a high degree of accuracy from a speeding jet moving at 2,500 miles an hour. But then he had something different in mind.

"Now, if I can just remember how this sucker works," Rock muttered as he slammed his hand down on a few buttons on the computer console. The screen in front of him suddenly filled with a video image of the runway, and they could see the planes below and the men running around by infrared detection. Rockson came in at about a hundred feet high and slammed the red FIRE button, then climbed sharply again, turning to the right. A rocket detached itself from beneath the MIG's right wing and soared down, leaving a white plume behind it.

They all heard the concussion as the jet hadn't quite cleared the area, and felt it shake wildly for a second. Below, a thundering explosion ripped the middle of the runway just as the first of the Russian jets, throwing on its burners, reached the now-smoking crater. It slammed into the hole without having gained any altitude, and like any vehicle that hits a pothole six feet wide and three deep—it dipped right into it with a grinding scream of wheels and metal. A nano-second later the craft erupted into its own little volcano of debris as yet another jet, unable to slow its takeoff, ripped into the flaming jet-cremation-chamber pit right in the middle of the runway. Only the third one was able to throw on its reverse thrusters, turn sharply to the side, and avoid exploding, running right off the blacktop and through a fence.

The Freefighters cheered lustily as they saw that Rock was as good a gunner as a pilot. There was no way the Reds could send up anything after them. Not off of *that* smoking pit! Maybe in a day or two, after they'd filled the crevice in and smoothed it over with bulldozers. But Rock's team would be in Africa by then.

"Son of a bitch," Sheransky muttered as he tried to calm his slamming heart. "You showed them a shit or two, heh?" he said, not quite getting the colloquialism right as he smiled broadly and slapped Rock on the shoulder hard. Which motion wrenched Rockson's hand from the controls for an instant and the jet swooped sharply to the right, dropping about a hundred feet in a second.

"Uh, pal," Rock said without taking his eyes from the console and the cockpit window, as he straightened the plane up and started regaining altitude. "Hitting the pilot is a big no-no. Nyetski, nyetski, yes?

"Sorry, Rock, got carried away," the exuberant Russian defector said, his face growing beet red. Archer—who had at last gotten himself strapped in, barely, as the belt was hardly made for a sixty-inch chest—laughed broadly. It was his kind of humor.

"Rock," Chen blurted out as he tore his face away from the side window. "Before we all start breaking out the champagne, I hope I'm reading that gas gauge wrong. Does it say empty?"

Rockson hit the gauge with his fist. It went to full. "Aw, it was just stuck," he said. "No sweat!"

84

CHAPTER TEN

Near the town of Jabal Al Uwaynat, right at the common borders of Egypt, Libya, and the Sudan, was located what had been termed many centuries before "The Bloody Triangle." There, countless men had died in ceaseless disputes and wars, and now four thousand more men gathered along the three hills that surrounded the field of rocks that were arranged in a bizarre swirling pattern—a pattern laid down by slaves thousands of years earlier, and long since disturbed by wind and storm. Their original outlines of lions, dragons, gods, and demons were hardly recognizable.

In the center of the rock garden a large winged stone sculpture crumbled at its outer edges, mutilated but for its wings and long serpent's tail. On its back, in a hollow twenty feet in diameter that had been carved out for ritual sacrifice, a fire burned, red flames rising up to the sky twenty, thirty feet. Men around its edges poured fuel on it and worked immense bellows so that the fire roared up at the dawn sky as if challenging the sun out of its cave of darkness.

The men on the surrounding hilltops were clad in myriad colorful and garish costumes: long, flowing robes of purples, oranges, greens, and golds. They wore beads and silver and jeweled necklaces. The men had proud, fierce faces of brown, black, cocoa, in which one could see the effects of their warrior genes. They whirled and jumped up and down, holding their spears and short swords, their ancient rifles, their shields made of elephant, zebra, and crocodile hide so thick and difficult for any blade to penetrate.

They lived to be fighters; they and their people had indeed fought for many centuries. And from the way each slightly differently garbed or beaded group glanced from hill to hill, it was obvious they were not used to being with each other. Each of these sturdy desert tribes was bunched together, separated from the other tribes.

The Libyan, Egyptian, and Sudanese desert fighters who had been gathered here were ancient enemies. Their fathers and father's fathers had murdered one another. Yet now they stood gathered together within spear's throw or rifle shot of one another. The tribes watched as the flames rising from a large pit on the back of the sacred sun serpent statue rose ever higher, beckoning the sun to rise as the stars quickly faded in the early moments of dawn.

Suddenly there were gasps and cheers from the assembled thousands as they saw a cloud of dust coming in toward them from the gray desert, beyond the half-crumbled gargoyle. It was *Him*—the Great One—the Man-God Kil-lov who had descended from the heavens to earth to carry out the prophecy. The Ka Amun. The Man-God who would carry out the prophecies of total rule, of conquering the world, of uniting all the tribes under the rule of his thousand-year reign.

As the dust cloud drew closer, they could see the priests of Amun walking in their long white robes covered with arcane symbols. They carried large religious symbols, carved from wood or chiseled from stone, aloft on poles. Some were heavy enough to take six, even eight men to hold them up.

On each side of the line of sun priests, drummers pounded out smashing beats on immense gazelle-hide drums which were carried along on straps around their shoulders. And behind them, other men blew on long brass instruments, sending out a cacophonous trumpeting of heart-stopping tones. The sheer spectacle of it all made the superstitious desert nomad warriors' bones tremble. If there had been any skeptics among the gathered about the power of the Amun cult, they were rapidly vanishing.

And suddenly they saw *Him*, in the center of the line of priests—the Man-God himself, the one who had descended from the skies on fire-feet and landed on the Great Pyramid of Cheops. The angel sent from the Sun God himself, a piece of the god, burning with Amun's unquenchable flame. Colonel Killov was carried atop a golden throne. He was dressed in the finest of Egyptian priestly garb—with long white robe adorned with precious jewels at every seam. A large triangular-shaped golden hat sat atop his head, and golden paint had been dabbed in hieroglyphs on his emaciated face and along his boney arms.

Ka Amun smiled as he saw the waiting army of fighters bowing down to him, screaming out their peculiar high-pitched wail of obedience.

It had been but three months now since Killov had parachuted from the skies but already, he thought proudly, he was rebuilding his empire—more powerful than ever. All that a man needed was his mind, and sheer utter determination. Not any man. Only one as ruthless and cunning as Killov could have come this far. Could have survived his parachute-burning fall from orbit. Could have survived three assassination attempts on his life since then. But then he had survived assassins even worse than anything these desert bastards could throw at him.

Tonight would mark the beginning of the next stage in his plans for conquest. This dawn he would expand his armies nearly twofold with the addition of many of the fighters around him, those who stood on the hills to see the Man-God. They would all join, of that he had no doubt. For he was about to give them a little demonstration of his powers. One they would not soon forget. And above all, men respected power. And obeyed fear.

Ka Amun raised his hands as the entourage came into the great rock field, and a roar went up from the collected warriors. At the very instant his hands, also painted gold, pointed up toward the sky, a blare of trumpets sounded again, and the bellows hidden behind the gargoyle blew harder so as to make the flames within the pit on top of it rise up in an almost blinding blast of white and yellow. At that very instant, the tip of the sun poked up over the far horizon, and another gasp went up from the masses. It truly *was* the son of the Sun. For he controlled its very rising. No mere mortal man could do such a thing. They prostrated themselves by the thousands, bowing and humbling themselves, hitting themselves with whips and chains on their arms and backs, to show their devotion before the Great One, the Ka Amun.

Killov was carried around the edges of the rock field on his golden sedan chair by a dozen Sudanese warriors stripped to the waist and crisscrossed with leopard-skin belts. He let them all see, feel his power.

88

Then he was seated in the center. He rose from the sedan chair and walked out, moving slowly, like a ghost, floating above the ground. And then he spoke. Killov had managed to get hold of a public-address system from one of the Russian outposts they had overrun a month before. A mini-microphone sat just inside his robe. Through wireless transmitter it was relayed to two loudspeakers hidden inside the chair that would make him sound like the Man-God that he pretended to be.

"Oh, followers of Amun," Killov screamed out, raising his arms high as if calling the sun to rise just for him. "I ask you to look up as my father, the sun, breaks from his death sleep and brings warmth and golden life to the day once again."

"Oh, Great One," they chanted back in English, the sacred tongue, the tongue of Amun, as they bowed even faster, rising and bowing down, smashing their faces into the ground so the Man-God could see their willing devotion, "speak to us!"

"I come down to earth—to free you. To free you from pain, from fear, from confusion. Now that you are to be my warriors, when you fight and die under my banner—there is only eternal salvation, there is paradise in my cleansing flames."

"Paradise," they shouted back en masse. "Paradise, Ka Amun."

"Yea, let the sun rise." He waved his hands at the sky as the high priests gathered around him, shaking their staffs and chanting various supplications for the sun to rise once again, a ritual they had carried out for over three thousand years. A ritual that always made the sun rise.

"Without us—without the Great Amun," Killov screamed into the mike as the words blasted out over the ears of the assembled nomad fighters, making them tremble, "there would be no sun. It would not rise. There would be only eternal night. And all would be cast into darkness, cast into a frozen death more horrible than the most terrible nightmares. *Bow to Amun!*"

"*Bow to Amun!*" the assembled priests screamed out as they formed a large circle around the Man-God and raised their staffs once again, as if supplicating the sun. And the burning orb rose higher, smoothly riding the morning breezes into the purple sky.

"Without *Amun*—you are worse than dogs, worse than ants, worse than lifeless sand," Killov screamed again, and the bowing masses pushed their faces even deeper into the desert, praying that the Great One should not catch their eye, should not single them out for his wrath.

"Yea, look up into the sky," Killov commanded. "Look up, up. See that sun follow the commands of Amun, see it rise to give warmth and life to the Sudan, to Chad, to Egypt, to the Earth itself."

"*See it rise!*" the assembled priests echoed out.

"And see this," Killov went on, as he raised his glowing red cylinder-crystal—the Qu'ul levitation-stick—and pointed it at three rock slabs each the size of a truck. "Raise your heads," the Man-God commanded the sprawled masses, and slowly, scarcely daring to, they lifted their heads a fraction of an inch at a time and raised their tightly squeezed eyelids. They weren't sure whether they dared look straight at the Man-God or disobey his orders. But they decided that it was better to obey, to overcome their terror and watch, as He commanded.

"Behold the power of Amun," Killov croaked out as he quickly popped down another Orbitol pill, one of the drugs the priests had been supplying him with. He had been up for days now, planning his campaigns, planning this event which would solidify a warrior army around him. But he was growing tired again. The Orbitol slammed into his sagging nervous system like a rocket and his eyes popped open, his heart quickened as if he was in a sprint. "See the power." He pointed the levitator-cylinder at the three clustered slabs of granite.

They rose up side by side smoothly, about ten feet apart, as the warriors cried out in awe. Killov, after his initial destruction of the Great Sphinx, had learned the art of the anti-grav device well. He had practiced with it night and day, wanting to be its master, wanting to be able to use it to fit his own designs. And he had learned well.

The three slabs, each big enough to crush a house, rose up and hovered over his head about fifty feet up. They began spinning each in a different direction like immense rectangular records on a turntable, not wobbling or shaking a bit. The desert warriors, if they had been frightened before, were positively shaking with fear now. Most of them had not seen the rock-flying powers of the Man-God, though they had heard about them. Some had scoffed at such a power. They didn't now. Tears flowed from their eyes to be this close to the Ka Amun and witness his miracles.

"Bring out the prisoners, the traitors," Killov screamed, and from a circle of priests in elaborate jewel-hatted garb were dragged out a dozen men all screaming hysterically. Their hands and feet were chained together.

"These men have betrayed the Sun God, have betrayed Kil-Lov—son of Amun," Killov bellowed. "They believed they could challenge my power." He laughed, a cackle that echoed through the hills and made even the priests of Amun shudder inside. The frantic, innocent prisoners were dragged forward to the center of the rock garden, where Killov stood. They were placed side by side, spread-eagled out along a flat rock twenty feet long, eight feet wide. Their chains were pulled tight at feet and wrists so they were tightly pulled down against the rock, unable to move.

"Now watch—watch and remember what happens to any who dare betray Amun," Killov bellowed into the mike, his eyes growing bright with the anticipation of pain. In fact, the twelve had committed relatively minor infractions—stealing bread or a pair of shoes, being several hours late for guard duty. But Killov allowed no mistakes, not one. And these would be far more useful to him as examples of his iron rule than their meager lives were worth otherwise.

He turned his hand, holding the glowing antigrav stick, and the three slabs over his head spun slowly away from him and right over the long sacrifice stone on which the sputtering and crying men were chained down.

"Oh, Sun God, we send more souls into your burning mouth," Killov intoned, and he lowered his hand. He moved slowly, not wanting it to be over too fast, and the three immense slabs dropped down an inch at a time as if on invisible pulleys. They reached the flesh of the men, and then slowly, terribly slowly, Killov lowered them further. There was a sudden chorus of terrible screams that even the highest on the hills could hear. Sounds that covered them with gooseflesh. And as they watched the slabs grind inexorably down on the chained victims, a wall of blood shot out from the sides of the rock-sandwich. Under such high pressure it gushed out a good twenty feet in every direction in a red waterfall spray.

Killov pressed the huge rocks down even further so they touched against the slab, and then he turned them back and forth like a man squashing an ant beneath his boots.

He let them rest there silently for a few seconds, and there wasn't a sound anywhere. Then he raised them up again, their undersides covered with blood. The nomad masses looked down breathlessly at the mess that was left behind. It was no longer recognizable as human. It was no longer recognizable as much of anything, really, beyond a tangled mess of red organs crushed like pudding dripping, and skulls and bones smashed into a wet dust. Nothing remained of the men who had disobeyed Him.

Killov raised his hand again, and now the killing rocks rose up over his head and began spinning like tops, spraying out the blood in a circle around him. Spinning like meteors, like red nightmares that would go into the dreams of all the men who had just witnessed the carnage created by Killov's very special weapon.

"Bow to Amun, swear to Amun," Killov bellowed out over his throat mike. "Swear your devotion, your allegiance, your willingness to die in his crushing army. Swear!"

"We swear our lives to Amun," the masses screamed out as one. Screamed out again and again, and bowed and prayed that he would not smite them. Killov smiled the frozen smile of a skull beneath his golden crown, and he smoothed his red-splattered finery. All the while, the three huge rocks spun just above him like the crushing fists of the ancient gods.

CHAPTER ELEVEN

America was a checkerboard of ugliness and beauty in ever-changing proportions from the air. Rock and his strike team flew across country in the MIG X7 trying to cloud-hop, so as to avoid radar detection. The Freefighters stared out the window in fascination as their great and wounded land whizzed below them. In some places there were just miles of seared black land, sometimes the color of charcoal, filled with craters. Vast wastelands of rad-death.

Because of N-Day, it was all dead, nothing growing even after more than a century.

Yet in other spots, America was beautiful, lush, filled with soothing greens and blues, the colors of the living earth, not of the dead one. The men's pupils alternately opened and closed as they passed over the different areas. Clearly the planet Earth was trying to heal itself, was trying to grow back in the many spots that had been nuked, burned, raped, mutilated. But it was just as clearly a tough job. Man had been an expert with death and mega-poison. His atomic weapons had killed not just other men and animal life, but the very flesh of the earth itself. Many of the wounds they would see would take a long time to heal—if ever.

"I just never get over it—what we did to the earth, to the Mother Earth," Rock said to no one in particular. "How could they be so fucking stupid?"

"The bad ones got control," Chen replied softly. "Just as they're trying to do again now. That's why we're even up here flying to the very ends of the earth. To stop it from happening again."

"Still, that's just a fact—it's not really an explanation," Rockson went on, grinding his teeth together. "What is it about man, about men? Do they have a fatal flaw that commands them to destroy—or was it just chance that the demented sons-of-bitches got control of everything?"

"A little of both, I think," Chen said even more softly now, so that both Sheransky and even Archer, who appeared to be listening intently, had to strain to hear the conversation. "The destructive bastards always try to get control. Men who lead are aggressive. That aggressiveness can drive them to the point of—madness, a lust for sheer destruction. And yet there are also more extreme men within that category of destroyers. There's men like Colonel Killov, for example. And then there's men like yourself, a leader, a preserver. Yet I know you kill, but you would stop fighting tomorrow and give up all your power, give up your rank in a second if the enemy were to cease his assault."

"You got that right, pal," Rock replied, wincing. "Give it all up. Then the whole bunch of us could just head out from that futuristic basement we call home and start some homesteads out there in the great radioactive outdoors. Be just like the old days. Pioneers, trying to reseed the country, make her whole again."

"I can just see Rona with the reins of a plow

around her shoulders out there in the fields," Chen commented wryly. "As you and her start your little farm! What exactly were you planning on growing?" The Chinese went on, unable to resist needling him.

"Avocados and pineapples," the Doomsday Warrior exclaimed, as if it were obvious. "They're in short supply at CC!"

"Meee liiikeee beee farmmmerr," Archer snarled out as the three of them laughed, a little surprised that he had understood the conversation. Rockson could never quite tell just how much the oversized near-mute really took in through those big ears of his. But he was definitely getting the feeling as he spent more time fighting alongside him that Archer was far more intelligent than his primitive speech, and sometimes equally primitive actions, let on. Who could figure it out. Maybe his IQ rose and fell depending on the time of the moon.

"It's the same in Russia," Sheransky said as he pulled his blond head away from the cockpit window, though he was fascinated by the jigsaw of death and life below. "Many of the common people—they don't want to fight. Don't even wish to occupy America, or any other land for that matter. They have no desire for an empire, just for their own little piece of the earth to grow food in. They want to own a small home, to have a family, children. It is the politicians who want only to further their own ends, who use the power to hurt others. I tell you, the common man—he is the same the world over. If we could just get rid of the damn bastards who run the show—maybe things would work themselves out all right. You know, like—burn all the kings and emperors and commissars and presidents. Then the rest of us could live in peace."

They were all silent after the little speech. In their

hearts they believed it was doubtless true. But such an event seemed, to say the least, unlikely. Still, deep inside, they looked down on the wounded earth that had given birth to all races and all living things, and they felt like crying.

They flew on through the early morning as streaks of light undulated above them in crazy patterns. The Aurora Borealis had grown dramatically in size and coloration as a result of the Nuke War. And in the century plus since, it hadn't diminished, but grown ever brighter, sometimes nearly lighting up the daylight sky as if with magnetic fire. It was a little frightening being up amidst the streaking rainbows of radiation. But though they felt an electric charge around their bodies, sometimes making the hair on their heads and arms begin to stand up when they went through a thick curtain of the stuff, it didn't seem to be doing anything bad either to the jet or them. But they sure as hell could feel something going through their flesh.

It was seven in the morning—and as far as Rock could tell from the onboard computerized mapping and direction system, they were somewhere over Tennessee—when the colors of the sky started turning a decidedly nastier color. The brighter colors of morning turned dark, deep brown, a blackish green, the colors of a diseased corpse. The weather-tracking functions of the jet's computer lit up, and warnings flashed across the screen.

"Something's up, Rock," Sheransky said as he read the Russian warnings that were coming in fast and heavy now. "Big storm coming up. It says we should get down, that the jet is not equipped to deal with—" Even as he was uttering the words of warning the jet was suddenly shaken around like a leaf in a rapids. They were all over the place,

97

spinning, twisting, rising, and falling hundreds of feet in a second. Rockson felt the craft go completely out of control, and tried to pour on more power to straighten her out, like a jockey kicking a skittish mount.

Suddenly the skies all around them turned utter black. Lightning was cracking, streaking everywhere in spiderwebs of white-hot fire. The men were too scared to utter a word, but held on tight to the sides of their seats as the jet went wild. It was as if they were in the jaws of a white shark and he was just ripping away, trying to get a good mouthful. Clouds the size of mountains formed out of nowhere and rippled with blue fire on every side, as if they were alive with electricity. In the lightning flashes Rock could see tornadoes dropping down out of the great storm clouds, snaking down to the earth below, wide funnels of black air which began sucking up whatever they could rip from the land.

Hoping to outrun the storm, Rockson poured on even more power as warning lights on the other side of the console snapped on, telling him he was approaching the danger point of the X7's power output.

"You'd better go slow with that," Sheransky shouted nervously as he saw the warning lights blinking. "It reads danger zone."

"I know what the hell it reads," Rock snapped back. It was clear in any language what was going on. The jet was going to come apart pretty soon, ripped open like a sardine can at the seams. He made a sudden decision, praying it was the right one, and slammed the controls forward, hitting the POWER OFF switch. There was a sudden eerie sense of motionless for a second as the g-force almost ceased. They could all hear the thunderous roars of the mega-storm outside and around them. And then the jet dropped straight down. Without power, it just pointed its spearlike nosecone toward the earth and hurtled down.

"*Shhiiiiiitttt!*" Archer bellowed out as they were all suddenly looking straight down at the cratered, lightning-illuminated ground. He clearly didn't like dropping like a stone from 65,000 feet. Not that the rest of them were too happy about the idea either, thinking that the storm had somehow caused a burnout in the jet.

"Rock—the power, the power," Sheransky stuttered out.

"I'm letting her drop," Rockson barked back. "It's our only chance. The electrical discharges were shorting her out. She just wasn't responding." He didn't add that he hoped he could get the engine turned back on again before they were mashed into steel sandwich spread on the hard earth below. But at least it pulled them out of the center of the raging storm. Even as lightning streaked wildly around them, as if trying to track them down and let them have it with a good 50,000,000-volt jolt that would incinerate the craft, they dropped right out of the clouds and down into the quiet dark air below that Rockson had hoped for. Even there though, the sky was filled with sheets of rain and hail.

Rock watched the altimeter and the ground too. He knew he had to time it all perfectly. There wouldn't be a second chance one way or another. The sheer speed and drop angle made it hard for the delta-wing aircraft to grab hold of the air. Still, they tried. Even within the steel frame of the jet, they could all hear the howling, angry winds outside like a million ghosts all knock-knock-knocking on their flexing door.

The ground was clearly coming up too fast. They could see trees and a road here and there. Could see them all too clearly. Rockson saw the warning light of imminent impact blinking faster and faster as the altimeter read out 3,000, 2,000, 1,000— There was no more time.

He slammed the POWER ON switches, waited two seconds, and when the engine whinnied into life, poured on everything the jet had. They could literally hear the craft creaking and making all kinds of awful bending sounds as its very molecular components were tested to their limits. A roar of fire poured out of the thruster of the MIG, and suddenly the g's were back in full force. The jet's nose swung up, straightening out as Rock pulled back as far as he could on the controls. He swore a pine tree's top just below them was going to take them out, but the jet just skimmed its needles, sending the top branches of the pine tree exploding off in flames. Then they were moving horizontally again. And they were alive, for the moment.

Rockson eased back on the controls, and the X7 climbed a few thousand feet until they were safely above the looming mountain passes. The storm was still roaring out its anger above, but the worst of the blow was much higher up, above ten thousand feet. Down here they only had to contend with driving sheets of rain that would have drowned the Ark.

"Good flying, Rock," Chen muttered from behind Rockson.

"Arrccchhheeer llooovve Rrroooccckksssoonnnn," Archer croaked out from his seat. Which made them all laugh, breaking the incredible tension of the last several minutes.

To Rockson's amazement, a tail wind from the storm aided their progress for a thousand miles, saving precious fuel. The mass-ratio computer reported that they would indeed make it to Africa, if they followed its "suggested" flight path.

They reached the long, curving shoreline of the Atlantic in just another twenty minutes without anything coming out to intercept them. Then the MIG left the land mass of America and they were out over the water. All eyes turned back to get a final glimpse of their home. All of them couldn't help but wonder if they'd ever see it again. They tried to shut up the dark voice inside that said "no."

Rock continued flying low, just yards above the ocean, creating a foaming furrow in the black liquid behind them. Fish, porpoises, whales floating near the surface looked up in fear, wondering if the sky was falling as the flaming thunder-thing passed overhead.

CHAPTER TWELVE

They flew across the great oceanic divide separating America from the other continents. Flew and flew, and flew some more. It was hard to believe there was this much water on earth, let alone in just one part of it. Sheransky got a game of cards going with Chen and Archer in the backseat, straining around in his co-pilot's chair to do so. Rock kept a firm eye on the console readouts and the curved violet-tinted windshield which almost matched the off-color of the smooth sea. Archer, tiring of the card game, fell asleep quickly, snoring loudly with his head back against the steel wall. Chen, who claimed he had never played Old Maid before, beat Sheransky game after game, until he'd lost every Century City dollar that he ever had or would have.

Rockson just let his mind sort of go into an all-systems-on, relaxed-but-ready kind of trance. He kept his hands firmly on the controls. He wouldn't even think of throwing her on automatic pilot and getting some shut-eye. Not for an instant. He just didn't trust machines when it came right down to it. Not more than himself and his mutant's sixth sense. No way, Jose. He'd stay awake all the way to Africa, then probably collapse as soon as he touched down. It was an eight-hour journey even in the high-speed MIG.

They were at about the two-thirds point according to the instrumentation panel when Rockson saw a warning that there were numerous large objects at sea level. He decided to go higher a few feet for safety, aiming the high-resolution video camera beneath one wing down at the water.

It was amazing—fish of all sizes and shapes floating on the surface all over the place. Many were quite large, twenty, even thirty feet long. They glowed, and it appeared that many, if not most, of them weren't moving. They were dead—and glowed as if floating in a radioactive sludge.

He scanned them, miles of them as the jet pushed on. Other immense sea beasts were snapping away at the glowing pink and green carcasses. And these feeders were equally ugly. Many really were more like oceanic reptiles than the fish he had seen in his time. A mix of shark and Plesiosaurs would about describe them. He thanked the Good Lord they weren't down there in a boat.

He cruised up to a few thousand feet, and stayed there for a good half hour watching the Sargasso Sea of Glowing Death, overwhelmed by the size of it. A whole portion of the ocean must have gotten poisoned as well as the land masses, Rock speculated. Somehow he'd thought that the atomic missiles would have hit only land. But of course a lot of them had probably misfired, or their guidance systems had gone haywire and they'd gone right into the oceans. Perhaps dozens of nukes had landed around here and killed everything. And over the century the radiation

103

had created the hideous sea creatures below.

Maybe it had even been done on purpose. Some madman on one side or another had decided in the final moments, "Yeah, we must poison the oceans as well so the enemy won't be able to fish from them." Well, they were right about that. Rockson wasn't doing any fishing around there.

He lifted the X7 higher, having had enough of the mutations, and leveled off at 25,000. There couldn't be any Red radar screens out here! Sheransky had fallen asleep as well, and his high-pitched snore contrasted nicely with Archer's animal slobbering sounds. Rock glanced around to Chen, who stared with almond-shaped eyes like clear black rocks in a stream straight back at him. A small grin moved across his face just for a second, acknowledging that he too had seen the feeding sea monsters.

At last as they rode out of the night and into the morning Rock got a reading that they were nearing land. They were over the Mediterranean Sea. He woke up Sheransky to help him with the whole series of instructions in Russian that were flashing on the jet's computer screen.

"It says, 'Approaching selected target area. Do you wish to arm nukes?'" Sheransky read sleepily, rubbing his eyes and dry mouth.

"Bombs? We have atomic weapons on board?" Rock asked with disbelief. It hadn't occurred to them that they were carrying anything more than a few conventional air-to-air rockets. If he had known, he would have dumped them to save fuel.

Ahead the sun was starting to rise, a burning ball floating up out of the perfect curves of the blue water, which ended abruptly, to reveal the great land mass of Africa showing up out of the haze.

"We still have about a half hour," the Russian

technician explained to Rockson. "But it wants to know if it should load our firing chambers with two small-yield nuclear-tipped missiles and begin implementing launching procedure?"

"How do you tell it no?" Rock gulped nervously. "Tell it to take all the nuke stuff out of gear and put it to sleep. Keep the other armaments, though. We may need them."

"Will do, Rock," Sheransky croaked as he hit the computer keys, one finger on each hand tapping out instructions fast like a woodpecker's beak. "There—done like you asked for." He smiled broadly, the wide ruddy face looking at Rockson with pride.

"I didn't know you knew about all this jet armament stuff, Sheransky. You really *are* handy," Rock said, somewhat amazed.

"Always try to pick up a few things here and there, you know. Hang out in the computer room at Century City a lot too. In Russia you better know *something* good when you come out of the army— or boom—off to the Gulags to pick frozen cabbages. So—" He shrugged his shoulders and looked at Rockson with a smirk. "I became expert-expert!"

"Listen, pal," Rock said, his eyes squinting as the north coast of Africa came fully into view. He could match it up against the image of the map on the monitor to his left. "Next time you know about something—tell me, man, you hear? I need every bit of information I can get my fingers on."

"Sorry, I didn't want to show you up or anything," Sheransky apologized. "In Russia, if you show you know more than the idiot above you—boom—you're licking ration stamps in Ikkutsk. I thought—"

"This ain't Russia, for Christ's sake," Rock said, exasperated. "I don't know what I'm doing half the time. We work as a team. Every man contributes what

105

he knows, whatever the hell it is. If you can tell me anything, tell me before—not after."

"Sure, Rock," Sheransky said sheepishly, turning and looking out the window at the coastline. Waves washed up on the shore in a foam of white that stretched hundreds of miles.

Whistling merrily, Rockson checked the fuel. *One minute's worth left!* Luckily they were very near their destination. His whistle stopped when he checked out the status of the landing gear. It was kaput. The right wheel had been damaged somewhere along the line. The readouts indicated it was leaking oil, its hydraulic system completely AWOL. He couldn't land on one wheel.

"All right, everyone, get your Soviet chutes on. We're going to have to jump. Sorry, but the party's over. Hey—are those nukes completely defused?" Rock asked Sheransky nervously.

"Da! The computer told me that the warheads are pulled away from the firing mechanisms on both missiles. It may cause some radiation leakage where it falls—but it won't go up and burn our tails, if that's what you're thinking."

"Well, I guess we're going to pollute an already polluted ocean a little more," Rock noted darkly. He dropped the X7 down, and slowed it, until the jet's computer indicated it was at optimum height for jumping.

"Everybody ready?" Rock asked, turning around in his cockpit seat.

Archer was still struggling with his chute, which Chen was helping him with after rigging it up with extra belt-webbing so it would fit around his broad shoulders. It would hold. But it looked pretty strange.

"Yeah, Rock," Chen shouted back as the sun came

106

from behind a cloud, streaming through the window, making them all wince even through the tinted glass.

"Your chutes will open automatically—or so they say. But the cord on your right hand side opens it as well, so—" Rock pressed a lever, and the canopy jumped off from the fuselage and flew away.

"How do we jump?" Sheransky asked as he looked from side to side. The jet's engine went silent.

"Oh, we don't jump." Rock grinned devilishly. "If I remember my manual—these are ejection seats." He slammed the INSTANT EJECT button. In a fraction of a second, with such speed that they swore they were all shot from a cannon, they were all rudely ejected out into the cold sky. None of them knew where the hell they were for a few seconds. They just tumbled end over end like clothes spinning around in a dryer. Chen came into a straight glide after about four seconds of freefall. Rockson an instant later. The other two Freefighters continued to flail about madly like birds with one wing for a few more seconds. Then all the chutes suddenly snapped open, timed to go after exactly eight seconds.

Then they were just drifting down, twisting around in the clear sky, marveling at the land below them and the sea just to their backs. And then marvel turned to fear as onshore breezes suddenly began sweeping them out toward the ocean again. Rock had ejected them when the console had said that the X7 was three miles inland, very near their rendezvous site. But quickly they were being carried out over the craggy shoreline, and then out over the water.

They all tried to steer their air-filled chutes. But although they held well enough, they were the old fully domed ones—not the cutaway steerable ones. Rock saw the plane fly on by, and slam into the water

107

two miles off, where he had aimed it. It slid smoothly into the ocean with scarcely a ripple, and must have gone straight to the bottom, for he saw no explosions.

Suddenly the dark water was coming up fast and Rock tried to steady himself for the splashdown. Landing a chute in water could be the last thing you'd ever try. He imprinted on his mind that his large knife was in his boot at his side, to know where it was once he hit, in case he had to cut ropes. And then he didn't have time to do any more planning. He came down feet first, and seemed to go down a good ten yards into the cold ocean before he felt himself being pulled back up again. Above he could see the chute, soaking wet, starting to drift down over him. If he got tangled in it—he was a dead man. Rock reached for the knife and cut the chute cords a few feet from the surface. He came up alongside it and threw his head up out of the water, gasping for breath.

Chen was already up, and then Archer too bobbed up like a big raft, his bearded face looking around frantically. Chen went back under, and came up a few seconds later with Sheransky, who spat out half the ocean as the martial-arts master helped him cut his chute free. Rock tore his eyes to the shore. They were about a half mile out. Not too bad considering.

"I think we can swim for it, all right. The tide's going in." Rock addressed the three of them as they bobbed around. God, wasn't this water cold for Africa, Rock thought. Too cold to linger in! "Chen, you keep an eye on our Russian friend here. I'll take the lead."

Rockson started ahead with strong firm strokes. Archer paddled right behind him. The big man could swim pretty good. He was splashing a little, like a moose in a tub—still, he moved. They had gotten perhaps a quarter-mile, nearly halfway to

108

shore, when Rock saw a motion in the water ahead, a sudden rippling coming straight at them from about a hundred yards off.

"Unknown something coming in at nine o'clock," Rock shouted to the others as he ripped out his thankfully fully waterproof shotpistol and kicked sideways away from the moving shadow.

"Holy shit," Sheransky stuttered, stopping his strokes, a few feet from Chen, who had been giving him an extra push every few yards. The shape came straight toward him.

"Move, out of the way it's—" Rock's voice stopped in mid-sentence as his tongue became instantly frozen by the sight of the huge head that broke the surface. It was like the rad-monsters he'd seen from the air. Only this sea creature was much uglier up close, and it was coming at them, opening its immense jaws. It looked like some spawn of Moby Dick which had mutated over many generations, and bore no resemblance to the more "wholesome-looking" fish of the past.

This one had spikes and bumps and rows of poisonous teeth all over its face. Its jaws poked ahead in crocodilian fashion a good thirteen feet long. It must have been sixty, even seventy feet from snout to tip of tail. Rockson knew such things had existed in prehistoric times. Shecter had told him many times about his theories of de-evolution. This ugly bastard had de-evolved his way back to the nastiest of the sea dwellers, back to before life even had time to get as pretty as the dinosaurs.

"Move, move." Rock suddenly found his voice as he saw the green eyes the size of truck tires zeroing in on the still-frozen Sheransky. "Move your ass, or it's going to be Russian stew for that monster." Rock raised his shotpistol as the huge head tore by about

ten yards away. He knew it was a puny weapon, but pulled the trigger. Then pulled again and again. The shots slammed into the side of the thing, and Rock could see little spurts of blood here and there. But it didn't hurt it—and it sure as hell didn't stop it.

Just as the creature came down with closing jaws, Sheransky kicked and splashed suddenly, coming to hysterical life as he tried to get out of the way. The thing went by him, taking off part of his jacket as a dagger-sized tooth sliced right down his shoulder and arm. The creature swam past them, chomping hard with its teeth all gnashing and grinding together like an oversized garbage-disposal unit. It took it about three seconds to realize that it wasn't eating anything but air, and it screeched on the brakes, turning around. The great flippers came splashing up out of the water, and then it was guiding itself back again, the thousand-toothed jaw opening wide.

Sheransky tried to kick his way out of the path again, but even as Rock swam toward him, he could see that the Russian was almost out cold already. And that he wasn't going to get to him in time. Suddenly Chen came out of nowhere, swimming right into the path of the creature. The huge head snapped around as the black-suited figure tore by it. The sea killer seemed annoyed that anything would dare swim into its view, and tore off after the new game. Chen paddled like he was on fire, and moved at high speed through the water with a kind of stroke Rockson had never seen. Still, the toothed face was gaining. There was no way even the martial-arts master could outswim something like this.

Suddenly he stopped in the water and spun around screaming out Chinese curses at the monster. Crazy, yet it worked, for the ocean mutant opened the big

110

jaws again, ready to take the splashing fool down into hell. Which was just what Chen had been waiting for. His hands flew inside his wet ninja suit and he ripped out two shurikens in each hand. Instantly all four were sailing out, whistling like tea kettles as they spun through the harsh morning light. They sailed right into the gaping jaws that were dripping seawood, saliva, and flesh from a previous meal. They went inside the creature.

Chen started swimming again the moment the starknives left his hands. And just in time. For suddenly, the whole front of the sea beast went up in a roar of fire. The jaws exploded right off the face, teeth, scales, flesh all pouring out as if it was a balloon that had been blown up too hard. A bunch of flying teeth came right at Chen like ivory shrapnel. He grabbed Sheransky, whom he had just reached, and dragged him under. They stayed down for a few seconds, and then he emerged again dragging the now-unconscious Russian to the surface.

The monster was dead. To say the least. Its headless body spun over and over in the sea, heading off to some watery grave as it continued to move without even the benefit of the small brain it had once possessed. A single huge eye bobbed like a buoy in the middle of a red slick. Rock caught Chen's attention and gave him the thumbs-up.

"I think you hurt it," the Doomsday Warrior shouted across to Chen, who was dragging Sheransky backwards, holding his head just out of the water. "I think you really hurt it."

CHAPTER THIRTEEN

They'd escaped, but Sheransky was seriously hurt. They all could see that once they dragged themselves ashore on a sandy beach. His arm had been ripped open. The flesh was gashed right down the middle from his shoulder almost to the elbow, a good three-inch-deep cut like a butcher starting to make the incision for the flank meats. He was out cold—lucky for him.

Chen took a vial from one of several packets attached to the belt around his waist and mixed it with sea water. Then he smeared the white paste all along the wound. It seemed to form almost a glue within a minute or two. Then he pushed the flesh together, and then wrapped cloth around it, tying it up the length of the arm. The wound seemed to cease bleeding so heavily. Sheransky was now conscious, but not too much, his head rolling back and forth as he moaned softly.

"Easy, pal, you're going to live. I promise you that," Rock said, laying a hand on the blond Freefighter's shoulder. Sheransky's eyes seemed to clear as he focused on Rockson.

"Yeah, sure I am," he whispered back through

pale tight lips. "I'm just faking it."

"We'll have to throw together a drag-rig," Rock said, looking around the shore and seeing nothing particularly usable. "I don't know how much traveling our friend here is going to be able to do."

"Carryyy?" Archer piped up, getting the drift of the problem. *"No! Meeee caaarrrryyyy?"* He looked imploringly at Rockson as if to say, "let me help out here, pal, let big, strong me make my contribution."

Rock pondered the idea for a few seconds. It would slow them down some, no doubt, but then so would dragging Sheransky on a makeshift travois. Rock scanned the shore back and forth, and then the skies above them. He didn't want to wait around here either. The Reds—or someone else—could easily have seen their plane go down, seen the chutes descending. There could be troops coming.

"Okay, let's try it, big man," Rock said. "But if he's too much for you—stop—and we'll build something." Archer scoffed at the idea that it would be too much.

"Meee carrrryyy moooosse onnnn baaaacckk." He chuckled effusively. Rockson would have liked to have seen that particular event. They rigged up a kind of backpack using Sheransky's Liberator rifle as a seat, and the webbed combat belt. Then Rock threw the whole contraption over Archer's shoulders, getting the Russian Freefighter up on his back. The thing looked ridiculous, and Sheransky didn't look all that happy hoisted up onto the near-mute's back like an Indian papoose. But it worked.

Archer had to lean forward, pulling with both arms at the straps to get the right leverage. But after he tested the whole setup, walking around in a circle for ten seconds, even hopping up and down a few times, it appeared that Sheransky's 175 pounds, plus

113

another 30 or so of gear, weren't about to present any major obstacles to a man who had carried a moose!

With Rock taking the lead and Chen the rear, they headed up from the shoreline and into the groves of palm trees that started several hundred feet from the water. Rockson was tense. He could feel his mutant senses all buzzing up a storm like a factory of alarm clocks going off. He didn't know the terrain here at all—and he felt something, something dark. It was indistinct. He wasn't even sure if it was nearby or far off. But it was somewhere around them, as definite as the very earth beneath his feet. He wondered if it was Killov's evil vibes, but again wasn't quite sure. Something, something bad, something that was only satiated with blood, and oceans of it, was around.

They made their way through the trees, which were closely bunched together—making the going difficult, especially for Archer with the heavy load on his back. Chen and Rock could duck down, but the huge Freefighter couldn't bend too far or even his strength couldn't hold up the load.

It wasn't really the trees that got everyone upset, but a kind of mutant dwarf palm bush that grew around the base of the higher trees. These were prickly, with purplish thorns, and gave off a pungent odor not entirely pleasant. Bugs seemed to cover the spaces between many of the thorns, and Rock saw some big orange and black spiders prancing around, checking out their sticky web traps. But they all seemed more interested in the bug world than the human, so after several minutes he relaxed, at least about the spiders.

It took them nearly an hour to make their way through the thick junglelike terrain. The trees seemed to get bigger and the vegetation leafier and thicker. The air itself became moist as a sponge, and

114

as the sun rose into the sky and heated up everything, the men felt as if they were inside a sauna. Rockson stopped every ten minutes or so to see how Archer was doing, but the giant Freefighter only grew annoyed as Rock stopped and turned each time.

"Noooottt ttiiirrreeed, Rrrooccck!" The Doomsday Warrior got the message after the third such response and didn't ask again. The air grew even moister, and the ground as well, so their feet started making squishing sounds with each footstep. And as they came around a mini-swamp with a family of flamingoes taking their daily dipping, Rockson saw why it was so wet. They had reached a river as wide and quickly flowing as the Mississippi, and dark colored, so that it was apparent there was much dirt and nutrients floating by.

Storks and pelicans and birds of odder species waded in the shallows along each bank, stabbing beaks into the liquid for fish—which they came up with on nearly every attempt. A rich and vibrant ecological system in full gear.

Rock knew what it was. He had read enough pages about it in the CC library, seen enough mummy movies to know. This was the Nile—in its full sweeping glory. The most fertile strip of land in all of North Africa, if Rockson remembered his geography and history correctly. The entire Egyptian civilization had basically developed along a narrow stretch of farmable land that ran along both sides of the majestic river. Ninety percent of her population through the milennia had lived within a few miles of the Nile.

They took a breather by the fabled river. As hot as it had been inside the junglelike forest, it was blazing out in the full force of the sun. But at least there was a breeze coming down the Nile, and the moisture there seemed cleaner, almost like spray from a shower. The rushing water was about a half mile wide where they sat in the sand.

Archer lowered Sheransky and sat down, taking a breather. He would never admit it, but carrying the heavy load in this kind of humidity and heat was already taking a toll on the Freefighter. Rockson knew the guy would go on until he dropped on his face, dead. He'd have to keep a close eye on him.

According to Rockson's calculations they were only two and a half miles from where Rahallah had directed them to meet him. It was near enough that he decided they'd march right up along the Nile banks to keep a little cooler than they'd be if they headed back into the jungle. It was more exposed out here—but at least no one would croak from the suffocatingly still air. He let Archer take ten, and then got them all moving again.

They marched past the water birds. The crocodiles floating serenely downstream seemed disinterested in them. But Rockson knew that they kept a beady eye out for anything that strayed too close to the water.

They'd gone perhaps two miles, and Rock was beginning to wonder where all the humans were since there was clearly plenty of animal life around. Then he saw several boats coming down the river. They were primitive things—long papyrus rafts with men poling their way along. The rafters eyed them suspiciously as they passed by about a hundred feet from shore, in the calmest and shallowest part of the river. They were dressed quite crudely, wearing what looked like hardly more than burlap bags cut into shirts and pants. There were about ten brown-skinned men to a raft, and they were carrying stacks of odd-looking vegetables. These were not dissimilar to bananas, but purple-skinned and much larger.

The boaters pushed their rafts out a little farther as they drew near, obviously nervous about Rock and his team.

Archer waved benignly, glad to see that there were human beings in what he had already decided was quite godforsaken country. But the boaters didn't return the gesture. They just poled out even farther, staring back at the Freefighters as if they were a landing party from Mars. All eyes were on them, heads turned around in their neck sockets, until the boaters disappeared around a bend in the river a half mile down.

"You ever get the feeling that you were a freak in a circus?" Chen shouted up from the rear.

"Since I was born," Rock quipped back as he turned to see how Archer was doing. Sheransky was looking paler by the hour, but the bleeding seemed to have stopped completely—which was the most important thing. He'd have to hang on. There was no choice. They had nowhere to go until they made contact with Rahallah. This wasn't exactly the kind of territory where you just drove up to the nearest hospital and pulled out your Blue Cross card.

They marched another forty-five minutes or so, until Rockson saw a landmark perhaps two miles to their left out on the jungle-bordering desert. It was something that caught his attention: three stone mounds, each about fifty feet high and shaped somewhat like ice cream cones that had partially melted. Rahallah had told him in the coded instructions that they would be met three miles up the Nile from the Mediterranean Sea, on the far side of the trio of ancient shrines to the Cat God, Omasis.

"That's it, boys," Rockson said, pointing over toward the crumbling shrines. They were so disintegrated now after the passing millennia that it was hard to tell that they'd ever been statues of cats—or that they were manmade at all and not some termite mounds long since abandoned by their micro-citizens. He steered them away from the river, and within a few hundred yards, once they had gone through a dense grove of shore-lining trees, they could feel the heat from the beating sun as if they were inside a blast furnace. Rock noted how the reeds and green growth that ran parallel to the river on both sides disappeared abruptly once they reached its edge. Back in America he was used to abrupt changes in vegetation patterns. But here it was alive with all sorts of life, and then *boom*, it was desert, all within the space of perhaps twenty yards. Just sand with nothing growing anywhere. They could have been suddenly dropped down onto the moon for all there was to see ahead of them.

Although the three crumbling stone monuments had seemed just over the hill, once they hit the moving sands the going was rough. It was like stepping in place—feet sinking in several inches and the body hardly moving forward, however much effort one put into one's legs. It took them nearly an hour to go the mile and a half to reach the sides of the three monuments.

They headed on past them, as Rahallah had instructed, marching into what seemed like endless rising dunes of yellow. Rockson couldn't help but wonder if they were heading into some sort of trap. If Rahallah *had* suckered them into something, they were going to have a harder time getting out of it than they had walking in. But he trusted the nobly born Rahallah. Rock felt that, inside, the African was basically a good man. He was trying to influence the Soviet premier, as his closest confidant, toward the side of life, not death. Anyway, it was sure as hell too late now to be having any second thoughts!

They reached the rock-strewn field that Rahallah had described. It was recognizable by the fact that rocks were sprinkled all over it, in a roughly triangular shape—a distance of about five hundred feet on each side. From the totally rounded edges of the stones and their ghostly white faded appearance, it looked to have been laid down thousands of years ago. A football field for the early pharaohs? Rock wondered. The Mummy Super Bowl four thousand years before prime-time TV? If so, this was a quiet halftime. No players on the field. And no bands either!

Rock and Chen helped Archer get Sheransky down off his back harness, and laid the man down. The Russian Freefighter was out cold now, and Chen sprinkled some water on his face and lips as they rigged up an umbrella out of one of Shecter's reflective blankets. They all sat down on the rocks, their buttocks instantly warming up from the sealed-in heat, and waited.

They didn't have long.

"What the hell is that?" Chen blurted out as he put his hands over his eyes as a sun-shield, trying to see off into the distance. It was hard for any of them to see at first as the heat fog was rising everywhere, making the whole desert around them shimmer and almost seem to move, like the surface of a wind-rippled lake. But as they watched, they saw that something was indeed coming their way—and fast. A cloud of dust was rising up above the approaching shape—whatever the hell it was.

"Dust tornado?" Chen wondered out loud.

"No, it's men—and I'm not all that sure they're friends. I can sense a lot of violence," Rock said nervously as he glanced down at Sheransky. "Maybe we should . . ." He looked around. There really wasn't a hell of a lot of cover, unless one was a sand beetle and could dig straight down. "Maybe we should head back to that broken-down trio of cat condos back there. At least it would offer some maneuvering." He turned to see how far away the eroded cats were—about five hundred feet. They seemed way too far suddenly as the dust cloud grew larger and came right at them.

"Let's move, man," Chen said as the dust swirled up into the burning sky. They got Archer loaded up again fast and started trying to double-time it back to the three fallen mounds. Suddenly the dust storm was moving very fast, and as Rock squinted through the heat haze, his eyes widened in shock. If he wasn't going completely blind or mad from the sun—a definite possibility—it was a herd of elephants. A half dozen of them were tramping along as if they were in a race for the finish line at the Jungle Olympics. Even as he watched he could see there were men riding atop them on shaking platforms made of reed and papyrus.

"I don't think we're going to make it," Chen screamed out as he ran right behind Archer, pushing him along with a hand in the middle of his back. "Should we prepare for defensive-spread formation?" But the question was hardly out when Rock saw that not only were they not going to reach the cover—but that they didn't have time to get any kind of fighting formation set up either.

For the elephants were suddenly out of the heat-haze—and coming straight at them at full charge. He could hear them now honking up a storm like a flock of deranged geese. The sounds were dispiriting, for the animals were clearly trumpeting out that they were the most powerful mothers around—and that anyone who had any ideas of messing with them could forget about it here and now. Rock could see now as the elephants drew closer that each of the somewhat ragged, rocking platforms atop the beasts held four men. A driver sat atop each beast's immense neck and directed it with a long slim stick. The other platform riders were carrying spears with odd-shaped two-pointed heads. But what amazed Rockson even more—as the huge beasts of burden barreled down—was that their trunks had futuristic glinting metal devices poking out from the ends of them, as if they'd been surgically implanted.

Even as he hesitated, unsure of whether to have his men run or fight, the elephants split into two groups of three each, and within seconds had effectively surrounded them. The huge beasts stood about ten feet apart and faced right at the four Freefighters, their massive gray trunks flailing about. Rockson raised his right arm to show he was there in peace, but the motion apparently frightened the honcho on top of one of the oversized animals and he poked the beast in the neck with the riding stick. It lowered its trunk toward the Freefighters, and Rock could see now that the metal device was truly attacked to the trunk surgically, with wires and diodes jammed in all over the place.

Suddenly there was a blinding flash of purple light, and as Rockson jumped back startled, the sand just a yard or so in front of him was hit by the light beam from the metallic trunk-device. It melted instantly, forming a pool of sizzling superhot crystal blob, a bubbling lava-like glass that he could feel the heat from. The man atop the elephant's head raised his own arms and yelled down something that Rockson couldn't understand a word of. The other beasts turned their trunks as well in their direction and aimed downward toward the four—but held

121

their fire.

Chen caught Rock's eye for a second and made the hand signal meaning, "Let's get it *on*." He reached slowly into his sleeve for some shurikens that could blow a man's chest into pickup sticks. They might even damage an elephant. Might. But Rock made the counter-signal to "scratch it." He glanced at Archer, who was also preparing to make a fight of it, but was not in a position to do so with two hundred pounds on his back. Besides, against these mega-monsters with purple lasers implanted in them, they'd be microwaved to charcoal in about a second flat.

"No," Rock said, looking at Sheransky, who could barely roll his eyes open to see what was up. They'd have to hope for a better chance later, when they weren't directly confronted by twenty tons of angry meat and tusks the size of sofas. He prayed he was making the right decision. "We'll surrender."

CHAPTER FOURTEEN

"I think he's trying to say, 'Get up on the elephant,'" Chen said as Rockson looked up, perplexed at the screaming black elephant-handler twelve feet above him. One of the elephants was brought forward, and Rock winced as he swore it was going to disintegrate them all with the beam weapon embedded in its trunk. But at the prodding of its handler, it got down on all fours and waited patiently. It had a rickety platform like the others, but there was no one in it, just the "driver" of the beast, who was perched forward atop its head, his legs draped down over its immense tent-sized ears.

"Well, I guess we'd better do what he wants." Rock gulped as he looked into the cold eyes of the elephant, which was waving its strange weapon-implanted trunk around like a conductor's baton, ready to strike up some bloody music. Rock prayed the creatures never got the notion to use the things on their own. God only knew what might make an elephant mad. But the handlers seemed to have the beasts under firm control, kicking them in the ears and poking them with the guide sticks to make them move. The Freefighters walked the few yards to the kneeling elephant, which kept looking at them out of the corner of its eye, and mounted up.

It was a tight squeeze with Archer, and Sheransky, who was now unconscious again, had to be propped sideways. But they fit—and the driver sitting ahead of them tapped the elephant on the side of the head, and it rose with surprising speed. Rock glanced around at the inside of the platform they were riding on. It was woven from some kind of reed like a wicker chair, tightly meshed, about an inch thick, and clearly quite strong. The material gave a little as they moved, but he could see that flexibility would be a virtue on top of a rocking and bumping elephant. Anything really firm would probably have cracked after a few weeks of use.

Their elephant was marched into line with the others, three in front, two behind, the armed riders letting their prisoners know that they were being watched at all times and shouldn't even think of trying to escape. Rock studied the men as the elephant line picked up speed and began heading right back out into the desert, seemingly into the middle of nowhere. The riders were a cocoa-skinned group, with proud angular faces and straight-looking Greek-type noses. They wore gray and light-brown robes that stopped at the knees, with geometric designs covering them. Atop their heads they all wore what Rock could only think of as a Napoleonic-type tricornered hat. But it was made of gold, hammered into shape. He knew they were wearing some sort of padding underneath the hats, for no one could have endured the metal hats touching directly against their skin under the stern gaze of that burning North African sun.

The elephant men watched the Freefighters as well, looking around at them, studying them like bugs under a microscope, not even pretending to disguise their abject curiosity. Were the looks saying, "Aren't we going to have fun cutting off your balls!" —words which Rock had seen in the eyes of other groups which had managed to take him prisoner over the course of his violent lifetime? No. Maybe they were sent by Rahallah after all. Yet if so, why didn't they say anything friendly, or act a little friendlier? Why did they come in on the charge, ready to melt anything in sight? And those weapons! How the hell did a primitive bunch of elephant-riding nomads get hold of such advanced technology? The questions flew through his skull like a swarm of stinging wasps.

Whatever and wherever their destination was, it didn't seem to be getting any closer. The elephant caravan just headed straight across the sand as it swirled around their tree-trunk-sized feet. From a good fourteen feet up where the Freefighters were located atop the woven platform, they could see for miles. But there was nothing to see but more white desert and the rising curtains of heat.

Rock was impressed by how easily the elephants traversed the sand and the dune slopes. He would have thought them not suited for desert travel, but their huge feet, which acted like snowshoes, spreading their weight out enough so they didn't sink in all that deep, and their tremendous strength allowed them to move along as if they were cruising down a four-lane highway.

As the afternoon wore on and the sun grew even meaner, Rock reached around to take out a few things from his hip pack. The driver saw or sensed the motion and shouted, reaching back with his long two-pronged spear, which stopped just inches from Rockson's chest bone.

"Just taking out something for him," Rock said slowly, moving his hands in slow motion as well. He pointed to the ailing Sheransky, and slowly took out the folded aluminized Shecter blanket, showing it wasn't a weapon as he unfolded it. The elephant driver let his beast move along on full auto and kept the spear hovering just over Rock's heart as he watched with curiosity and not a little fear. The unknown is always fearful to men, even if it's the peeling of a banana!

Rock got the thing unfolded, and with Chen's help spread it out over the prone Russian Freefighter, covering every part of him, even his head. The driver suddenly grinned as he realized what the function of the glittering blanket was, and smiled at Rock, the first time any of them had done anything friendly—which gesture encouraged the Freefighters a little. The driver pointed to his own metal hat and nodded, saying something totally incomprehensible to all of them. Then he tapped the side of his head and nodded approvingly. In any language that was clearly translatable as: "That's using your noggin."

The elephant caravan marched through the burning afternoon—if anything, picking up speed as they really got into their full open stride. Again moving slowly so as not to alarm anyone, Rock and the others took out food pellets and water from their packs. But as long as they did nothing too fast and showed their driver just what was being taken out, he allowed them to get what they wanted and move around within the confining papyrus-wicker platform with its surrounding three-foot-high walls.

Archer started getting a little moody after a few hours—he hated being confined, and apparently didn't much care for riding elephants either. He kept grumbling, which grew louder as he shifted around,

126

more and more ill at ease—which the driver began getting as well when he saw the commotion. But Chen rested a hand on the giant's shoulder and talked softly to him, calming him down after a couple of minutes. Archer buried his face inside a corner of the reed platform and made low gurgling sounds.

Rock checked Sheransky every hour or so, and decided he had to change the man's bandages around mid-afternoon. The elephant ride and its rocking, jarring motion as each large foot came crashing down had gotten the bleeding going again, even with the glue-like suturing of Chen's miracle salve. The two men pulled back the Shecter blanket and took a look at Sheransky's wounded arm and shoulder. It was bad. There must have been some sort of poison or high-rad toxic chemicals which the mutant fish had injected into the wound, for it was festering quickly, and had already turned a vibrant purple color. Rock swore he could almost see the damned thing throbbing. Whatever was happening was happening too fast. At this rate, the Russian Freefighter wouldn't make it more than a day or two.

"I'm worried about him, man, really worried," Rock said to Chen, who cleaned the wound as best he could with canteen water, and then put more of the white salve all over it. The color seemed to subside slightly, and the tension in Sheransky's face relaxed just a touch.

"We can only do our human best," Chen said softly as he bandaged up the wound again with fresh cloth and then set the Schecter space blanket back over the man. "The rest is fate." The talking caught the driver's attention and he nodded vigorously, pointing ahead with a broad smile on his face and slapping at his arm.

"I think he's saying—there's help ahead," Rock

127

CHAPTER FIFTEEN

They marched on into the night, the great bull elephants with their tusks like immense sabres of bone glowing white in the light of the crescent moon and the trillion-starred heavens. Rock was awed by the beasts. It was a powerful feeling to sit atop one and feel its strength pounding through the sands. He could see why the handlers of the great proboscidans sat tall and proud, with looks of supreme confidence. Up here on one of these suckers, with its destructo-beam snout, there probably weren't a hell of a lot of things that could take you out, even in this eerie wasteland of a world.

They had reached the end of the desert, at last. Rock kept a sharp eye on their surroundings, trying to pick up the slightest object that could be used as a mark later, in case of escape. A tree here, a moldering palm that had fallen over on its side, the carcass of an elephant—this one perhaps only a child, as it was but half the size of the monster he was riding. Anything that he could file into his mind for the return trip. Sheransky was out cold, even with the bumping ride. Archer slept through it all, his head back against the side of the mini-cabin in the sky. Chen, as usual, was taking his own silent notes with half-shut eyes, seeing everything.

Around midnight, as Rock looked down at his weather-, earthquake-, and acid-resistant longitude-self-adjusting combat watch to see just what time it was, they heard a thundering noise coming far from the west. It sounded like great booms, mountains falling atop one another. Rockson had never heard anything quite like it, even in a few major earthquakes he had lived through. Even the handlers lost their look of ultra-confidence as the elephants themselves grew agitated.

But they drove the beasts harder, and the sounds seemed to diminish as if going past them far off, perhaps twenty, even thirty miles away. Rock felt a terrible premonition deep in his chest. There was a feeling so dark contained within the sounds. So final! Then the thunder died out completely. Still, Rock swore he could feel the very earth move, right up through the elephant's bones.

Rockson awoke with a start several hours later. He had fallen asleep despite his best efforts not to do so. He heard a sound, and turned to see what had awakened him. It was almost dawn. They had marched all night. They were approaching a village or—something. He rubbed his eyes as it looked most peculiar: tentlike structures in the shapes of small pyramids, ranging anywhere from ten to thirty feet high. They stood in concentric circles, nearly a hundred of them. They had to take up ten acres or more. Yet because they were covered somehow with sand or a sandlike material that coated them completely as if glued on, they appeared almost invisible. Rock realized that they were trying to hide themselves from aerial detection. From a few thousand feet up, these mounds were just more dunes in an endless, shifting desert. Even ground troops would say the same, unless they came very close. And with the heat put out by the sands, even the body heat of their inhabitants within would be concealed from infra-red detection.

Two guards stood on each side of a road that ran into the tent compound. Next to them were the same plastic devices that the elephants had in their trunks. Only these gleaming death-ray shooters were mounted on tripods, set up like machine guns.

The handlers of the elephant caravan waved and uttered some words. The guards laughed and stood up on their toes, trying to peer into the center elephant's basket to see the prisoners. They waved the men through, the lead elephant stepping inside just as the already blazing sun broke free of its nightly hiding place and lit up the whole scene with eye-searing light and heat. When it got hot, it got hot fast out here!

The inhabitants of the hidden tent-city wore the same garb as the elephant men, the same steel and gold tricornered helmets, and had geometric patterns that looked like hieroglyphs covering their short robes. Some wore armor on their chests and backs. Suddenly Rock realized what it was he was looking at: an army. This wasn't a civilian village but a troop camp. Somebody had gathered together a lot of men. And, as he passed a long, flat sand-covered tent-dwelling hundreds of feet long, he saw elephants in roped-off stalls inside. Man, they had enough mounts to carry a good deal of the mini-army to war!

They came to a higher, double-pyramid-shaped tent with connecting tunnel between the two halves, each half about twenty feet high. This tent structure was surrounded by men dug into trenches with all kinds of weaponry poking out. They were protecting somebody who carried mucho weight around here.

The elephants came to a stop right in front of the place, and Rock's elephant again kneeled down. The driver turned and started yelling at them in that sharp, almost clicking language. It was like no other Rock had ever heard, even with his years of study of language patterns in Century City's linguistics class—a must for a world in which on every mountain they spoke a different language. But this one sounded crazy, hardly related to modern tongues. Like it had evolved before modern language patterns had started to develop.

The Freefighters dragged Sheransky off the beast, and suddenly Rock saw the sand-coated tent material part like curtains in one of the pyramid shapes. A tall black man, very strong, stood there in a metal breastplate oufit. Rockson's face lit up with optimism for the first time in twenty-four hours. It was Rahallah.

"Rockson," Rahallah said as he came forward with a concerned look on his ebony face, seeing that one of them was hurt. "I'm afraid there's been a terrible misunderstanding. These men weren't supposed to attack you, but to bring you back here. Their squad leader, the only one who knew the exact situation, was bitten by a rad-wasp along the way and died within hours. I hope my—my men didn't do that to your Freefighter." Rahallah spoke anxiously as he kneeled down and looked closely at Sheransky.

"No, it happened when we had to eject from our jet and landed in the ocean. We were attacked by something that should only be in horror movies."

"He's hurt badly," the black man said, his full-lipped face and wide brown eyes looking in full concentration at Sheransky's face as he pressed his thumb against the man's neck artery. "He's in

132

trouble. Lost too much blood. Bring him quickly into our headquarters.''

A tall mocha-complexioned man came up. "Rockson, this is Tutankhamen, the head of the whole army you see here," Rahallah said as he rose. "He's a good man—and on the right side. The side we're all on, pledged to stop Killov no matter what the cost.''

"Any man that's an enemy of the colonel is a friend of mine," Rock said, holding out his hand. He took notice of the man next to Rahallah for the first time. He was about fifty, with closely trimmed silver beard and hair, very firm square jaw, and the same burning eyes as Rahallah. He reminded Rockson instantly of drawings he'd seen in books of the pharaohs of primordial Egypt.

The man smiled and held out both hands, covering Rockson's, an act of warm acceptance. "Honored that you have come all this way to help us," Tutankhamen said. "You and your fellow Freefighters are welcome to all that is ours. Among my people, we share everything. You are of my people now.''

"You speak English," Rockson said with some pleasure. It would sure make it a hell of a lot easier to communicate with him than the clicking, all-consonants dialect that the elephant drivers spoke.

"English is the language of the gods," Tutankhamen replied, bowing toward the east. "The high priests of my people and I, those of us who must communicate with the gods, may speak in their language.'' Just how laser-carrying, elephant-riding Egyptian pharaohs spoke English with a decidedly Oxford accent was something Rockson would ponder much later.

"My home," the pharaoh king said dramatically, his arms high on each side as if he were acting out

133

the part of Moses, "is your home. My food, women, hunting dogs . . . You shall consider them as yours, to do with as you want to. And now, while Rahallah attends to you and your men, I shall see to my troops. It is hard keeping so many warriors caged up like this. You, Rock-son, are a great general, I've been told. You would understand. But we've waited. Waited for your advice on how to take on the dark one's forces. Waited for your help. There can be—no mistakes."

He turned and walked off with half a dozen heavily armed guards walking on all sides of him, hands on the curved razor-sharp swords which sat in jeweled sheaths at their sides.

"This whole thing is like Ali Baba and the forty thieves," Rockson exclaimed to Rahallah as they started inside the twin tents. The black man of royal African descent had been kidnapped by Russians when just a child, Rock knew, and brought to Russia, where through the strange twists of fate he had become first Premier Vassily's servant, and then, over the years, his most trusted confidant. Rahallah now wielded immense power. In his own way, nearly as much as the premier himself. Which many in the Kremlin didn't like, to say the least! There had been numerous attempts on his life, from explosions to poisons and everything in between. But none had succeeded. The black man was as strong both mentally and physically as Rockson himself. In all the world, Rockson knew that this man alone equalled him on *any* level of combat. He prayed they'd never have to fight against one another.

"Here, we must work on this wounded man immediately," Rahallah exclaimed. "I'll take him into my private medical chambers through the connecting tunnel. Why don't you and your men go into this room over here. There's food, bathing, sleep."

"They'll go," Rock said, motioning for Archer and Chen to take ten. Both obliged, walking in, Archer yawning loudly and scratching himself like a flea-bitten bear as his nose began wriggling around his face, smelling food ahead.

"But I'll come with you," Rock added. "I'd like to keep an eye on just what's going to be done to him. You don't mind?"

"Not at all," Rahallah replied as he carried the 175-pound Sheransky along like a large rag doll. The man had muscles like anacondas stretching beneath the steel meshed robe.

Rockson asked, "Who is your doctor?"

"I'm the man who's going to treat him. I'm a doctor, Rockson, in both Western medicine, and with my own tribal brand. I've developed them in a symbiotic way over the years, mixed them together. I promise you—it will help him."

"He's in your hands, pal. Do your thing." They walked into the second tent, and Rock's eyes opened wide when he saw what the inside of the tent was made of: elephant hide, stretched out on joined-together tusks of the whitest ivory. Evidently, these warriors had learned to use every part of the beast. It was perhaps the only way they could survive the hardships and barrenness of such a desert as surrounded them!

Rock was a little taken aback when the uncon-scious Sheransky was placed atop a long slab of wood, obviously a makeshift operating table, and Rahallah stripped down to leopard-skinned loin-cloth. The African ripped out two rattles, gourds with beans inside, which he proceeded to shake violently as he jumped up and down and raced

135

around the prone body of Sheransky like a wild man. Rockson tried not to react. Maybe there was something in it all that he couldn't fathom. The man was clearly not a charlatan.

Rahallah, his broad ebony face covered with sweat as he moved around, took out some powder from a skin bag and threw it over Sheransky's head and chest. The powder was colored brown, black, and bright red, like blood. He nearly covered the stripped-to-the-waist patient with a thin layer of the powder, as if he was trying to bury him in sand at the beach. And then Rahallah began to howl at the top of his lungs:

"Oh, Lion God, please come and hear me. Save this wounded man. Give him the power of your beating, unstoppable heart. I, Rahallah, son of the Plains Lion, son of the Father of my tribe, beseech you. Let me hear your roar, Lion God. The roar that frightens even death."

Rock stepped back, startled as Rahallah's whole face suddenly tightened up into a snarling demonic appearance. Rahallah let out a roar that nearly gave his observer a heart attack. Then another higher-pitched roar as the black man reared back and then forward, screeching right over Sheransky's motionless body. He did a complete go-round of the table, roaring like a lion with its ass on fire, and then stopped in his tracks.

"That's the first part of the procedure," he said, turning toward Rockson with just the hint of a smile. "Now the second part." He quickly stepped back into his Egyptian fighting armor and sandals, and then walked back over with a small mobile table with one of the beam weapons atop it, and bandages and salves all over the thing on shelves.

"These lasers are not just for destruction," Rahallah said as he picked a bronze-looking laser tube up and switched it on. A beam of light—blue and hard to look at, so pulsing was its perfect blueness— came out a foot and stopped. It actually burned the air as it heated molecules of oxygen in infinitesimal pops from the super-heat. "The lasers can be used for healing, Rockson. The heat of the sun is contained within this little beam. You saw what the beam could do."

Rockson looked on anxiously as Rahallah lowered the beam-weapon toward the Russian Freefighter's wounded arm and shoulder. He trusted the African, but . . . Sheransky's face would be smoking ash if he made the slightest error in judgment. Rock tensed up, but he didn't say a word or move a muscle as he was afraid he might distract the "doctor." He just prayed real hard that Rahallah knew what the hell he was doing.

Rahallah lowered the blue laser toward the flesh, and with an incredibly deft touch, sliced it along the outside of the bandages, cutting them open like a razor, without touching the flesh below. He pried along the cut and looked in at the wound. "You've cleaned it well. That's good. I'll just use some of this—and—" He reached down and sprinkled liquid from a jar on the mobile table throughout the eight-inch wound, which Rock could see extended right down into the bone. He winced. He had never liked to actually see what was inside a man's flesh. Although he sure as hell had seen it enough times.

Once the wound was thoroughly cleaned, Rahallah brought the laser tip down to the wound and inside it. There was a puff of smoke, which rose up out of the wound, as he pulled the laser quickly across it. Then he stopped, looked down, and started over again.

He was sealing up one layer of muscle at a time. Rock had witnessed a kind of laser surgery once back at CC, but nothing like this. Rahallah was sewing the different layers closed with burning stitches with the expertise of a Hong Kong tailor. It took him only five minutes. And the wound was sealed with a burnt white line about a half-inch thick that ran the full length of the arm—closed with its own flesh as a bandage.

"Amazing," Rockson said as Rahallah at last stood back, let the laser die, and let out a sigh of relief that it was over.

"I think—he'll survive. That scar won't look too great—but—I haven't had any plastic surgery courses lately."

"He's not looking to win any beauty contests," Rockson said. He suddenly felt terribly tired, as if he needed to sleep now that all the tension was over.

He'd been out in the sun too long, on the elephant too long. In the jet too long.

Rahallah had to grab him as he fell. "Quickly, put this brave man in bed," Rahallah snapped. A dozen servants rushed to obey.

CHAPTER SIXTEEN

Rock awoke the next morning refreshed, finding himself on a long plush couch with a stiff animal-smelling blanket thrown over him. He remembered he had awakened once and eaten like a pig—and then passed out again! He got up, and was pleased to find that there was fresh water in a small bowl to wash with and to clean out his stinking breath. He'd forgotten his toothbrush, but his finger would do.

"You are look-ink for toot-brush?" a voice said hesitantly. Rockson turned to see an absolutely gorgeous raven-haired woman with high cheekbones and voluptuous rouged lips. She was beautiful, and wore only a flimsy pink robe with the same odd hieroglyphic symbols all over it. She held out a small toothbrush and a towel, and smiled coyly. Rockson couldn't help but grin.

"If it's going to be this much fun waking up every morning here, in wherever the hell I am, I'm going to stay here forever." She giggled and raised her hand to her mouth, making her firm melon breasts, just barely hidden inside the gown, shake alluringly. Rock held his temptation in check. The man who had just come all the way from America to help guide the entire Neo-Egyptian army against Killov couldn't just jump back into bed at the slightest provocation, could he?

He just took the toothbrush, not her. Rockson brushed his teeth and splashed some water on his face and neck. Then he got dressed, blushing a little under the watchful and appreciative gaze of the young woman.

"I'm Neferte," she offered.

"And I'm Rockson, Ted Rockson. Rock, my friends call me."

"Rock," she said, rolling the word over her tongue in a most provocative manner.

"Oh Lord," Rockson mumbled under his breath, and headed outside. The first thing he wanted to do was find out just what the hell was going on. He and Rahallah really hadn't had a chance to discuss the situation and all its ramifications. He saw two elephants waiting as he came through the flap. Rahallah was sitting atop one, the other was empty. Rock gulped.

"Ah, there you are, Rockson. I wanted to let you sleep—yet I wanted to be here the moment you awoke. We have much to talk about—and very little time." He shouted some sharp words to the second elephant, and it kneeled down.

"He's your war elephant from now on. His name is Kral, in the closest approximation in English," Rahallah explained. His English was filled with high British overtones as he had learned the language at Oxford in Britain, where the premier had him sent when in his late teens. Rahallah, among other talents, had turned out to be a scholar, and had majored in languages.

. "*My* elephant?" Rockson echoed dumbly back. He walked hesitantly over to it as the immense half-

140

armored animal turned its head and looked at him, not too overjoyed apparently with what it saw.

"He's a full battle-class elephant, old and scarred. He carries total body armor—and a Class A laser cannon. He's tough, all right. Just be nice to him and—"

Rockson jumped up atop the bent leg, and then grabbing the ear as he'd seen the others do, he pulled himself up by swinging onto the broad neck. The beast roared out, its trunk snapping up, and the whole back shook for a second as if it was thinking of throwing him off. A bucking elephant, that's just what Rock needed right now.

"No! No!" Rahallah shouted over. *"Never* pull the ear of a prime bull elephant! You must grab the hair on the back of the neck near the ear, and pull yourself up."

Rahallah gave some loud orders to the creature in Egyptian, and it suddenly stood up, whipping its snout around to sniff at Rock, who tried to seat himself comfortably atop its broad neck on a padding of cloth.

"Just sit back on him and sort of nudge him this way or that by moving your leg. Prime bulls think they know it all—and they probably do," the black man said as he started his beast forward. "They pretty much take care of you. That's why I gave you this one. There's no time for you to learn to ride a younger one, they need more training. This one belonged to a general—he knows his job. Just don't pull his ears."

"Never again," Rock said, raising his hand in Boy Scout promise as the elephant did indeed start forward with a loud harrumphing sound. The beast pulled alongside Rahallah's animal, and they moved slowly down the main central clearance of the vast camp. Rock, evidently, was being shown around.

"These are all fighting men here, elephant divisions, infantry. They're combat hardened—and ready to do whatever is necessary," Rahallah said. Rockson could see that there were indeed acres of the troops. Men everywhere were practicing their fighting techniques. Some were doing sword work in long lines facing each other, first one side striking—then the other. Blow, counter-blow, counter-counter-blow. They looked as though they knew what they were doing.

Another group about fifty yards down was working with their long double-edged spears with fluted, almost hooklike ends that looked as if they could just rip apart anything that they touched. They practiced on stacks of thick palm trunks that had been set in the earth in holes. The swords were slamming into them, slashing away and ripping even these foot- and two-foot-thick segments into pieces in just a few blows.

But it was the sight ahead of them as they came over a dune that really caught Rock's full attention. Two whole cavalries of elephants charging toward one another, their riders' arms outstretched with long spears, slashing away at the air. There must have been fifty or more elephants on each side, all of them immense bulls in full body armor—steel mesh that came down around their legs and flanks. The elephants' heads were helmeted as well, each one of their helmets a different grotesque shape. Welded out of solid metal, they formed hoods and death masks. Spike-augmented tusks were poking forward beneath the head armor.

The two groups came unceasingly toward one another as they waved their trunks, and man and animal alike screamed up a storm. Yet as they came to each other's lines, the ranks somehow passed through, spears just missing opponents by inches.

"They're just training—war games, I think your colloquial American expression goes. As if war could ever be a game."

"Jesus," Rock said as his mouth dropped open in amazement. "Who are those elephant fighters? I mean, where did this whole wild operation come from?"

"It's a typically bizarre story, as are most in the post-nuke world," Rahallah answered as they moved on to see yet more training facilities on both sides of them. "Somehow, remnants of the Egyptian army survived a few nuke strikes during the Great War a century ago. A bunch of them, nearly five hundred, survived intact. Because these men were in the midst of their own desert-war maneuvers, they found the cities destroyed when they went and looked—but some areas around the pyramids were untouched. So there they developed a culture, out in the desert, where the sand at least was less radioactive than the rest of their nation. They had been out testing very rudimentary weapons using lasers as mere sighting devices, nothing like these weapons of ours! But it was a start. Slowly, they adapted to what was around them, began dressing in the styles of the ancient pharaohs they found in the vast burial chambers unearthed by quakes, adopting their ways. The only culture that survived the war—as amazing as it is—was the truly ancient culture of the pharaohs. They just bypassed all that man had wrought for about five millennia—and started over."

"But these weapons—and the elephants!"

"The weapons were developed by a group of scientists who had been along to study the laser-sighting weapons—several Americans, the rest Egyptian. They—and their children—continued to develop the lasers and enhance them. They learned to

143

attach them to some elephants they had captured and trained. Out here in the shadows of the tombs of the pharaohs, they continued to develop their entire Egyptian culture. These are the Northern Egyptians —now inhabiting the banks of the whole northern part of the Nile. Killov has captured the Southern Egyptians—the followers of the Sun God, Amun. That is how he is spreading his dark words of destruction—as the Angel of Amun, as His Son, descended from heaven. An angel of death pretending to be one of life! And they believe him, or at any rate, they are too terrified to disobey. Already, he has taken two countries—the Sudan and Chad, and a good portion of Egypt! Libya may be his by fiat if the tribal leaders who are meeting today decide to surrender."

"But how can he convert people so fast? I mean he doesn't exactly have the pleasantest of ruling philosophies."

"That's exactly it," Rahallah said from atop his rocking elephant. "His weapons are far more terrible and planet-threatening than even these laser weapons. Somehow Killov has acquired—through the priests of Amun who now comprise his top leadership and military staff—some kind of devices that can levitate things—huge rocks, whole small mountains. He can raise them and smash them down on man and beast alike. He has killed thousands, perhaps tens of thousands already! He cares nothing for human life. Nothing—crushing whole villages like ants. That's exactly how he rules, Rockson— through sheer unbridled terrorization of the populace."

"Sounds like the Killov I know and love to hate," Rockson said bitterly as his elephant let out a long gooselike honking sound. He wondered if he had done something wrong again.

"Killov hasn't been able to find us out here in the middle of the desert so far. But that's not for lack of trying. He's had his units out all over the place, on search-and-destroy—the Southern Army uses camels and horses for that. He threw a few planes at us, but we managed to shoot them right out of the sky, as they were old props. So, for the moment, he's confined to the ground. That's our one bit of good fortune. He has to track us to find us. My general Tutankhamen has moved the camp five times in the last month. It's all extremely mobile. But it's only a matter of time. I know you have waged large-scale battle operations. I remember reading the reports that came in on the premier's desk for many years of one Rockson victory after another against some Red Army convoy or battle group.

"In spite of myself, I must confess I always felt a certain admiration for you even though you were always the 'enemy.' Against vastly overwhelming manpower and firepower you seemed to manage to come out on top. And when we fought alongside one another for peace in Washington, I was *honored*."

"*I'm* honored," Rock replied, "but I must admit to being a little—make that *very*—apprehensive now." Rock looked over at the black man. "I've never fought in a desert terrain like this—and I've never fought atop war elephants that could give King Kong pause to think."

"Yes, King Kong," Rahallah mused as if off in his own thoughts for a moment. "Excellent movie, excellent. Not the re-make, of course! Nonetheless, you have carried out large-scale combat maneuvers involving tens of thousands of men at a time in your career, if I'm correct."

"Yes, I think it's been known to happen," Rockson

145

said, a dozen memories of a dozen battles rushing through his head.

"Well then, you're ahead of the rest of us. I know it will involve strategy, not just head-on collision with the Killov forces. We know—because several elephant battalions, nearly a hundred Class A elephants, have died, with five hundred men. This army looks large—but it's perhaps three thousand men, no more, and barely a thousand war bulls. But if you see Killov crush an entire village with one of his damned levitating mountains," Rahallah said, his voice suddenly growing cold and filled with rage, "you know we must act immediately.

"He is worse than any man," the African prince went on. "The way he kills is not for power, nor wealth, the way other men kill. They at least can be controlled, bought off, so the human race can survive. No, *he* kills for pleasure, just to see it, to experience the pain and the agony of others!"

Suddenly Rock's gut was filled with the most chilling sensation, as though he were going to puke out some of last night's massive dinner, which was still digesting in his overfilled stomach. These men, the whole stinking country, all of Africa was counting on him, and he didn't even know how to make the damned elephant he was riding go to the left or the right!

CHAPTER SEVENTEEN

Rock inspected the rest of the camp as Rahallah led him on out through the concentric circles of sand-covered elephant-hide tents. There were four sprawling circles of them, encompassing the entire fighting force of General Tutankhamen's warriors. Rahallah wanted him to see everything so any decisions Rockson made regarding their ultimate strategy would be made with complete knowledge of just what there was to work with. It was clear that the African didn't want to take the responsibility for the large-scale operation solely on his own shoulders. Not many men would. Not that Rockson looked forward to being responsible for the life and death of thousands of men, not to mention the whole continent of Africa. But the difference, perhaps, between Rockson and other men was exactly in the fact that he was willing to shoulder the decision-making, and to take the risk of total failure.

They toured the encampment for nearly two hours, going up and down every dirt passageway between the tents and covered trenches. Some "roads" were so narrow that the huge elephants could barely fit through even single file. Rockson was quickly getting an immense respect for the multi-ton beasts. They weren't just huge—but smart—and quite graceful, all things considered. Nimble enough to get through passageways between sand dwellings with hardly more than inches on each side—doing it without sending any walls crashing in. He'd like to see one of them in a china shop. Rock's beast, Kral, seemed to settle down once it got used to him being up top. And once it saw that he was basically going to let it do the steering. It's like that in any marriage, too—compromises have to be made. And the Doomsday Warrior wasn't about to argue with something that outweighed him by twenty to one.

Rock filed away everything he saw in his brain. He still hadn't the foggiest idea of just what he was going to do against the Skull, but at least the information was being fed inside, where he could feel it all whirring and clicking into the right slots. He just prayed they had enough time to work something out. If Killov attacked immediately, was able to break up this force into smaller groups, send them on the run in all directions without leadership, it might well be all over before it had begun.

He banished such thoughts from his mind. Yet within his heart he felt a certain fear, a feeling that he hardly dared acknowledge. A fear that Killov was not human, that the Skull truly *was* in league with darker forces.

The man should be dead by now. By all rights he *was* dead. Killov had been killed more times than a nine-lived cat—and still came back. Somehow each time he was more powerful and threatening than ever.

This time Rock would make sure the bastard was terminated. He would stand over him and see his flesh and bones placed deep under the dirt. And then would wait a few hours just to make sure the KGB colonel didn't crawl out again. Seldom did Rockson feel such an animosity, such a loathing for any living thing. But Killov was not of the living, as far as he was concerned. Rather, he represented the dead, dark forces of the universe. Surely the man had been born from under a rotting log along with the scuttling bugs and larvae. It didn't seem possible that he could have sprung from a human womb, from a human mother.

At last Rahallah told him that that was it. There was nothing else to see as they reached the very outermost sand tent a good half mile from the center of the circles of bivouacs where they had started. He led Rock back down one of the wider paths to the center of the camp, and stopped right in front of his own double-tent headquarers. Rahallah tapped his elephant on the side of the head, and it kneeled down on its front legs. He jumped down onto one of the great tusks, and then to the ground.

Before Rock could say a word, his own war bull was down too, and Rock imitated the black man. Not quite as successfully, as he nearly tripped, getting his foot lodged somehow between tusk and trunk. He reached up, grabbing instinctively for the huge ear hanging down like a round theater curtain. And even as he made contact with it, grabbing hard, he suddenly remembered it was a no-no.

The elephant let out one of its patented trumpet blasts sure to wake the dead. But whether it was a tribute to its training, or whether it was already getting used to the moron who was riding it, the great aimal didn't drive a tusk through Rock's chest or lift him in its multi-yard-long trunk and throw him halfway to Timbuktu. It instead let him regain his balance on the tusk, and then jump to the ground hard. But Kral did give him a look like a shark staring at a minnow that had swum into its view.

Rockson grinned sheepishly and mumbled a few inane words.

"Sorry 'bout that, big fella. We don't have elephants—in America." Then he shut up as the beast's squinting eyes narrowed even further. It clearly didn't want to hear any bullshit.

"Come on, Rockson," Rahallah said, amused but not showing it beyond a slight uplifting of his lip. "Let's check on your wounded compatriot. The danger period will either be over—or he will be heading into death—irreversibly."

Rock didn't like the way the man was so cold about the statement. Yet it was undoubtedly true. Perhaps it was better to think like that, without sentiment. Just the facts. The truth was truer without sugar-coating all over it.

They walked into the field hospital where Sheransky had been transferred the night before from Rahallah's special "treatment" room. Rock prepared himself for the worst as they walked through small elephant-hide-walled rooms where fighting men in various states of dissolution or recovery lay on papyrus hammocks swinging slowly back and forth. But he wasn't prepared for what he saw as they came to the end of the sand-floored corridor and turned right. In his own private room lay Sheransky, surrounded by nurses who were giggling and making quite a fuss over the "wounded" Freefighter. He was puffing on an immense cigar and pretending to blow smoke out of his ears, eyes, and other parts.

"Rockski—hey, what's up, pal?" Sheransky said with a broad, beaming smile on his face. Food trays and empty cups lay around the bed, and it was one-hundred-percent clear that the man was in his element.

"Jesus," Rock mumbled as he walked to the side of the hammock while some of the squealing nurses— actually young women hardly out of their mid- teens—went rushing around the bed and the Russian Freefighter slapped at firm young buttocks, eliciting yet more squeals. "You're looking fitter than a fucking fiddle."

"Whatever you did for me—by Lenin's balls—it worked," Sheransky said with some amazement, slapping himself on the chest. "I swear I was standing right in front of the dark door—and it was opening. But then—I wake up here where there's food, beautiful women! I'm feeling like I'm seven- teen again. Maybe I should get clawed by high-rad fish every day."

"Thank Rahallah here," Rockson said, resting an arm on Sheransky's shoulder and looking down at the man with a warm feeling in his guts. He had been dead sure the bastard was a goner. One case where his sixth sense had erred—thank God.

"Thanks, mister," Sheransky said as he turned and looked at the black man, who stared back down impassively. "I—I appreciate your saving my life. I wish there was some way to repay you since—"

"Please," Rahallah replied, raising his hand with a mild scowl. "Enough said. Just your coming here on such a treacherous journey to help us in our hour of need is far more than I could ever repay. It is nothing."

"Well, that nothing happens to be my life," the Russian defector answered back enthusiastically. "And I'll tell you the truth—it sure as hell matters to me!"

Rahallah shooed away the coca-skinned nurses. As

151

they rushed away, Rock admired how their skimpy swirling gowns of green and purple flowed around their perfect young bodies—and almost envied Sheransky.

Rahallah opened Sheransky's bandages so he could get a look at the wound. He examined it closely, pinching the flesh lightly between his fingers here and there, squeezing the already hardening scar tissue from the laser tool as Sheransky let out sharp barks of pain a few times.

"Excellent, you're doing extremely well. Better than I had hoped," Rahallah said as he stepped back.

"So I can get up and out of here now, right?" the Russian Freefighter asked with a broad grin, though just why any man would want to get up away from those doe-eyed, firm-fleshed nurse-ladies was something Rock couldn't quite fathom.

"No, at least another day, maybe two," Rahallah said, firmly. "My medicine—antibiotics mixed with traditional African medicines—sometimes can do great things. But not miracles. Only the gods can perform them. You were very close to death, my friend. Closer than I let on even to Rockson here. Your body is healing—but it's still in a state of shock. I'll check you again tomorrow."

"Ah, Rock," Sheransky said, looking over at the Doomsday Warrior like a little boy who wants another cookie, "I want out."

"Forget it, mister," Rockson said, trying to make his face firm, but letting a narrow grin trickle through. "He's the boss here. Besides, with all the babes you've got running around in here, I figure you'll need at least a day or two just to get things sorted out. I never knew you were such a ladies' man."

"I guess I figured all those American karate gals

152

back at CC would kick my butt if I grabbed for anything. But here . . ." He glanced around with a dreamy look on his ruddy face, and suddenly realized that maybe it wasn't the worst thing in the world to stay in bed a few more hours. "Well, I guess I'll survive." And with that, the girls were back and all over him again, kissing, pinching, grabbing. Rock shook his head as he and Rahallah left the room.

He checked out Chen and Archer, both of whom had apparently found things to occupy their attention. Chen was being shown the Northern Army's unusual laser-weapons and demonstrating some of his own. Archer was out demonstrating his crossbow on targets hundreds of yards away. Rockson retreated to Rahallah's headquarters, where they went over maps of the whole of North Africa. The black man showed him where Killov had struck already, where his forces were believed to be concentrated, everything that a general would need to know to plan a campaign of counterattack. But by the end of the day Rock was more confused than ever, and hadn't even begun to get the slightest inkling of a plan to go against the colonel. Neither had General Tutankhamen.

"Let's stop now," Rahallah said sometime after dark as Rockson was bent over yet another map, staring at it as if in a hypnotic daze. "Too much concentration can make a man go mad. Come, Rockson, tonight we have prepared a little banquet for you and your men. It is the least we can do to show our gratitude."

Even as Rockson opened his mouth to protest, Rahallah turned down the oil lamp in the map room and nodded for his guest to follow. Rock shut up and walked after him. He couldn't even tell what he was looking at anymore. A respite would be nice.

But he was hardly prepared for the dancing and drumming, the horns blowing, the elephant-hide rafters just about falling down!

Rahallah had led him several hundred yards to a low but quite wide and long sand tent. The place was rocking. Rahallah grinned at Rockson's double take. Clearly he had been expecting some rather more low-key meal with an extra date or two, not the free-for-all that was being played out within. Men were dancing on tables, flipping over each other's heads. In the center of the floor barely clad maidens were undulating out the Dance of a Hundred Veils—and most of their veils were already deposited on the floor.

And the food! Rockson could smell it even as they walked in. And as he saw the whole goats and cows turning on huge spits and being basted with spices and honey, saw the vats of nuts and fruits and the table filled with gourd vessels of homemade beer and wine—Rock knew he'd come to the right place.

He was seated with Rahallah on one side and General Tutankhamen on the other. Young women greeted him enthusiastically with wet kisses on both cheeks and multitudinous expressions of joy at his attendance. They all sat on firm silk cushions of brilliant coloration, and as Rockson looked up and down the table, he saw Chen and Archer at the far end, about thirty feet away. Their hands were filled with food—their mouths as well. Both spotted him and waved with crazy smiles on their faces.

"*Goooood*," Archer screamed out above the din of the goings-on. Rock had barely gotten himself comfortable when food was thrown down in front of him. And thrown was the word for it. Whole sides of lamb, their juices dripping, gourds and bowls filled with yogurts and cheeses and fruits, and alcoholic concoctions Rockson couldn't even begin to imagine the ingredients of. He took a deep gulp of his fiery white fig-wine, and dug in.

It was delicious, along with every bite of whatever he tried. They sure as hell knew how to cook out here in the middle of nowhere. Maybe because there wasn't a hell of a lot else to do except count the sand grains.

As he ate, the place seemed to grow even wilder. There was a whole band of drummers on one side of the thirty-by-hundred-foot sand tent. And they were banging away at trees, stones, logs, all kinds of things, creating a cacophony of sound that took a few minutes to get used to. But once he did, Rock could hear that it was a mix of complex rhythms all blending together into one great motion of sound. The sound of the rhythms of life itself. Or—he was getting drunk!

Warriors with their fierce nomadic faces and hieroglyphs painted all over their stripped-down sweating bodies were spinning around like whirling dervishes, racing around the center of the place which had been cleared for dancing. They leap-frogged and did somersaults, performing feats of amazing agility and gymnastic prowess. First one group, then the next. At first Rock thought they were all the same—but he saw after a few minutes that they had slightly different colored beads and body paint. They were probably from different tribes. Tribes that had perhaps once battled one another in the past— but now lived and fought together under the banners of Tutankhamen's Northern Army. Now they competed against one another in dance and song rather than bloodshed.

Rockson stuffed his face with something from every platter and goblet that was brought before him, realizing as he ate and drank just how much tension he had been storing up in his body. He felt himself getting more than a little drunk, with everything spinning slightly in a pretty nice way. But as the saying went—eat, drink, and be merry for tomorrow you die. Not that he was expecting it—or wanting to die—but you might as well be prepared. A good meal to last an eternity. It was the least a man could go out with.

The evening seemed to get wilder as it grew ever darker outside, the dancing more frenzied, the food and fruits flying through the air. Then there was a momentary lull while one group of dancers left the center floor before the next had come on. Rock watched in amazement as he saw Chen and Archer both rise up from their pillows and come flying right across the top of the table out onto the rug-covered sand floor. Archer started to do some kind of insane jig, spinning his legs this way and that, like an Appalachian madman. Chen did back flips, forward flips, rolls, and wild twists as if he was competing in the Olympics. Then a kickoff, and he was soaring through the air right up on top of Archer's shoulders. Archer caught him up there, even as he kept his own wild leg-snapping dance going.

Rock shook with laughter as the whole place erupted in roars of approval and the high-pitched shrieks the desert people were wont to let out, like steam escaping from a kettle. That noise happened whenever they got really excited. Even Rahallah's usually stern and stoic face broadened into a wide grin, and then he burst out in belly laughs. Rockson wondered when the hell the two Freefighters had worked out such a mad routine. But as he watched on, taking a deep swig of a honey-flavored beer, he saw that they hadn't worked it out, for Archer suddenly tripped and went right over on his face, even as Chen flew through the air a good twelve feet, landing in a roll on the ground. But as the drums continued to pound and an off-key flutelike instrument rose above it all, swinging out an ancient melody, they were at it again, linking arms and square-dancing, down-home style.

Rockson started to get up to join in, his own inhibitions definitely getting lost in the shuffle of brews set before him. But even as he rose, ready to dive across the table and join in the fun, he felt a soft touch against his shoulder and the smell of a powerful fruity perfume that instantly sent his senses reeling and made him stop in his tracks.

Neferte. She had appeared out of nowhere, and instantly was cleaving to his side, rubbing her soft hands over his shoulders again and again with infinitely soft tugging strokes.

"No—do—do not go," she said in halting English. Then she smiled at him, batting her doelike eyes so that he felt himself nearly swoon with the power of the pure animal sexuality the woman was putting out. "You need—save energy for love!" She grinned openly, without shame or embarrassment about her desires.

Rock let himself be swept away by her warm softness and scent. He let himself be led up from the table as he saw everything revolving around him in a wonderful, dreamy kaleidoscopic way. Let himself be led by the softness of her hand through the back of the great banquet tent with nearly fifty upright tusks set all around the inside to hold it up. And out into the cool desert night air.

Then they were back in his tent, and she was all over him. She was like a cat, arching and mewing out little sounds that drove Rockson to the point of madness. Her smell was like the first ripe flowers and fruits of spring, rich and intoxicating. Her body was like a classical sculpture with perfect breasts which literally sprang out as she untied her skirts of silk. And then her pure softness!

It always amazed Rockson just how soft a woman can feel against a man's hard body. Passion was like fire licking logs, or water slapping stones. And he didn't know where the hell he was, except that it was somewhere near heaven. Heaven on earth.

CHAPTER EIGHTEEN

Rockson didn't know what time it was, or for that matter quite *where* he was. Just a world of perfect bliss somewhere between Coney Island and paradise. So it was even more unpleasant than it might have been on a normal night when he suddenly felt himself pulled out of the dreamy darkness of his sleep. It took him a few seconds, with the six glasses of liquor in his blood, and the hours of lovemaking having brought his body to exhaustion, to quite figure out what was up. There was a thundering noise, as if someone was slamming a sledgehammer right down next to his head. And he swore he could feel the very desert vibrating beneath him.

Rock opened his eyes as he felt Neferte's warm arms wrap around him. She muttered some words in her own language, which Rock couldn't understand but which were clearly utterances of fear. And even as he held her, listening for what in his dim state of mind he assumed was thunder from a passing storm, the elephants around the camp began letting loose with blaring trumpets of fear. The sounds increased by the second until the whole camp was alive with the thundering roars. Rock knew the animals were not easily spooked. They knew they were the toughest things around. So if they were scared—something was wrong, really wrong.

Neferte clung to Rock like a starfish around a clam, not wanting to let go of him, ever. She kept muttering "Qu'ul, Qu'ul." Rock remembered hearing the word the day before—something to do with the levitation weapons of Killov and his forces. Thundering rocks—the *Qu'ul!* He remembered Rahallah telling him! And suddenly his eyes opened wide and his heart was beating fast, all senses on full alert. It was one of the things he liked about his mutant nervous system. Even with hardly any sleep and a good quart or so of fiery brew in his gizzard— when the shit hit the fan somehow he was on all systems within seconds.

"We gotta move, babe," Rock said, suddenly throwing back the fur blanket which had kept the chill night air off them. "I pray I'm wrong—but I think Killov is making a move." They dressed fast and ran to open the flap of the sand tent. The camp was already in chaos as elephants were being led or ridden all over the place. Men were pulling down the ivory-tusk supports posts of their sand tents—the things were coming down everywhere he looked.

But it was the sight to the north that caught Rockson's attention. It was as if the sky had fallen to the earth and was churning up a caldron of steam and smoke of biblical proportions. Huge funnels of dust were rising everywhere as if a hundred tornadoes had touched down and each one was trying to wreak more havoc than the next. There was an immense cloud of dark dust which had risen to form a semi-globe over the desert a good ten, perhaps as much as twenty, miles wide. It was hard to tell just what was happening as the whole event was taking place miles

160

away. But it looked bad whatever the hell it was. And it was coming their way fast.

"Rockson, Rockson," a voice screamed down from a passing elephant that came to a lurching stop just yards away from him, its huge saucer eyes panicked and blinking. It was Rahallah, sitting high atop his war bull in full battle garb—sword slung around his shoulder and loose at his side, the long rifle that the officers carried, a blunderbuss of a weapon which Rock had seen take out whole palm trees.

"What the hell is going on?" Rock screamed up as Neferte came up behind him, tying her waist-long black hair into a quick ponytail so it wouldn't toss in the wind. "That's like no storm I've ever heard before."

"It's not a storm," Rahallah shouted down, his own face showing a stark alarm. "It's Killov—or at least some of his men. That's what happens when they attack. The smashing rocks create these huge dust storms. One of Tutankhamen's advance units— a party of twenty men on war bulls—went out early this morning to check the faroff sounds. *Two* made it back, barely, with their lives. They say the Killov war party is heading right this way. We have less than half an hour. Maybe *way* less. They can move fast on horseback. The men are breaking down all the tents—they'll be out of here fast. I'm heading out with an attack force of fifty war bulls with full battle-platform contingents to try to divert the Killov force—slow them down long enough for the army to escape. You can travel with Tutankhamen and I'll meet you at—"

"The hell you will," Rock screamed back up. "I'm coming with you. I didn't come all this way just to fly out of here with the old ladies, the pots and the pans. Where's Kral?"

161

"He's still in the pens. They're gathering them all to move them out en masse." Rahallah seemed to debate internally as he bit his lip hard, and then nodded to Rockson. "Get on, mister—we'll have to move. The diversion force is gathering at the north end of camp. They're moving out in five minutes."

"See you, toots," Rock muttered as he kissed Neferte hard on her still-sleep-puffed lips. She looked angry at him, but as a particularly loud thundering sound from the north shook the entire camp, her fear took over and she ran off toward the women and children. They were mounting up on large pack elephants loaded down with all kinds of gear. Rock had seen others mount up on the elephants without having them kneel, instead leaping up onto the tusks and then up to the neck and back. He imitated the motion—without grabbing hold of the great bull elephant's ears—and jumped along the animal's head past Rahallah, sitting down in the empty battle platform behind him.

Rahallah prodded the animal on the side with his guide stick, and it turned on a dime and headed back the other way, to fetch Kral.

It took only a minute or so to reach the large pen where nearly two hundred of the animals had been enjoying a calm night, munching away on palm leaves gathered from along the Nile. The elephant-handlers were already leading the immense beasts out from the pens with taut hide reins going from one to another. In small groups the animals were fairly manageable, but with numbers this large on the move, they got overexcited and could sometimes lose control.

Rock spotted Kral, and as Rahallah pulled up alongside him under Rockson's direction, he jumped right across the two yards separating the beasts. Kral

162

felt the weight of the man on his back, and looked around to see Rockson getting himself seated on the small saddle over the creature's neck.

The animal was clearly used to Rock already, for it didn't protest or even look at him funny.

"Let's *move,* man," Rahallah shouted. "If we're going to join up with the diversion team—we'll have to make time."

"My men?" Rock suddenly blurted out.

"They'll take care of themselves. The others will help them. I promise you they'll not be forgotten, even in the midst of this madness." Rahallah was right, Rockson realized as he tried to calm his rapid heart. Besides, he wasn't their dorm-mother. They were men, Freefighters. They had to be able to take care of themselves—and would. He was heading into becoming a fuddy-duddy in his old age if he didn't watch himself!

"Let's go then!" Rockson said, slamming both legs against the elephant's neck, not even caring if he angered the self-driving beast. There had to be a time for a man to take control of the animal beneath his legs—and this was it. Kral responded by moving fast, coming up alongside Rahallah's bull. He seemed to want to be guided tonight, to want to know that someone—even an ear-puller—knew what the hell was going on with all the thunder cracking in his ears.

They tore through the center of camp, heading in the opposite direction from where most of the people and other animals were heading. Rock thought he saw Archer riding astride one of the beasts, along with a half dozen other fighters, but only for a second. It was too dusty with all the commotion to see clearly.

When they were out of the camp and about a

163

quarter mile ahead, he could see the brunt of the attack force already tearing out ahead of them, heading straight into the dust maelstrom to the north. Rahallah shouted down into the flapping ear of his war bull, and the animal shot ahead as Rockson's mount followed suit, speeding up their great driving legs so that they created their own mini-thunder slamming against the desert.

Rock turned around for just a few moments to look at the camp. He could see a steady line of men and beasts heading out from the southern end. They were moving fast, hoping that enough time would be bought by the defenders for them to retreat safely.

The elephant men were fast—but then out here with the enemies they faced, you'd better be fast or the sand centipedes were going to have some extra helpings.

They caught up with the rest of the force, which was literally galloping across the desert. Rahallah's and Rockson's war bulls were clearly among the fastest, for they pulled even with the herd soon, and then moved up alongside it to the lead.

Tutankhamen's son, Ramses XXVII, whom Rockson had met briefly, was leading the charge. Unlike most armies, here it was expected that the top leadership would be right in the forefront of a battle, a fact that Rockson, as a long-time combat man having to deal with the chairbound leadership of Century City, noted with respect. Tutankhamen himself had reluctantly stayed to lead the main part of the army to safety.

Rock and Rahallah joined the younger man now. He was a fierce-looking bronze-skinned fellow, just inches short of Rahallah. Their three elephants synchronized their pace; they were moving at virtually identical speeds. Ramses raised his fighting spear high in salute to the two men's arrival.

It didn't take them long to reach the outer edges of the destruction that was being carried out. A cloud of dust suddenly enveloped them, and it was hard to see all that well, as if they were in a sandstorm. But as they came up over a high dune and reached the plateau, they could suddenly see for miles ahead—see the charnel grounds of death and total destruction. They could see the great "pounding rocks"—from the size of trucks to the size of buildings—rising up and coming down again and again like the boots of the gods, pounding the world into submission. What the hell could you do to fight *that?*

There were villages here and there around the desert ahead, and they were being pulverized, turned into powder—men, beasts of burden, huts, whatever. It was all smashed down to the sand from which it had sprung. Rock felt a sick feeling in his guts as he watched the rising and falling rocks doing their dirty work, their blood-pressing.

The Northern Army elephant force pulled to a halt just at the edge of the other side of the dunes which led down into the lush lower lands. The pounding rocks were now about five miles off and coming in fast, straight toward them. Ramses raised his royal baton and pointed to different sides, and the elephant force divided up into two groups, each twenty elephants strong. They formed up into a wedge-shaped force and suddenly went tearing down the long decline right into the storming hell.

"Point with the guide stick at what you want the elephant to fire at," Rahallah screamed out at Rock as they galloped side by side straight toward the conflagration. Rockson reached around and grabbed hold of the long, elaborately carved guide stick, and watched as Rahallah and Ramses began firing. They did so by catching their elephants' attention, then reaching down and aiming their guidesticks along the trunks so the elephants could see them—the beasts would point up at the target indicated. It was the beasts, amazingly, that actually controlled the firing. A mechanism within the trunk was twisted so as to activate the lasers.

Rock wasn't even sure they could reach that far, but as the other war bulls opened up, he saw that the lasers' light-beams held an absolutely straight path all the way to their targets, not wavering a millimeter. Still, the sheer mass of the immense boulders and rocks ripped right out of the earth made even the laser weapons, which had previously seemed completely awesome to Rock, now appear almost like peashooters.

Some of the smaller levitated boulders *did* erupt in explosions of dust and fire. But the large ones hardly seemed bothered by the blasts, turning around slightly, but not disappearing, not by a long shot.

Rock's bull tore ass alongside Rahallah's and Ramses's mounts, all three elephants raising their trunks, firing and then firing again. Between the dust of the stampeding attack force and the dust that came ever closer from the anti-grav'd boulder mass, the whole world became hard to see, as if a carpet of night was being laid out over the desert.

The worst of it was that even when they managed to destroy one of the smashing rocks, they really hadn't hurt the controllers of the levitation sticks—who all rode on camels a mile or so behind, according to Rahallah. Thus they were only getting the shells as it were—not the cannons themselves, or the men who were firing them.

Rock could see quickly that they were in trouble. Against an ordinary army the laser-equipped elephant force would have been a formidable adversary. But against the potent weapons of destruction Killov's Southern Army wielded, their diversion force was laughable. He suddenly started getting a real sick feeling in his chest, as if something terrible was about to happen.

When it came, it came with such speed that there wasn't time to react. All of a sudden out of the sandstorm that swirled around the desert, amidst peals of thunder as if the earth itself were shattering, came a building-sized chunk of debris right at them.

Rock and Rahallah were just outside where the crunching stone fist hit—but Ramses and about six other elephant-riders were not. Rockson saw them disappear beneath the crushing avalanches of rock, and didn't hear even one scream. There wasn't time to even know you were dying when one of those suckers hit.

When the boulder rose up again, there wasn't a trace of men or beasts. Just a crater in the desert going down a good six feet, and a red slime that coated the surface sands throughout. It wasn't fair.

"This way, this way," Rahallah bellowed out over the din of battle, and Rockson, without a second thought, turned and followed the man. Or rather his war elephant did, for the beast could see the tide of battle wasn't going their way at all as well as any. The two men rode hell-bent for leather as their charging bulls let loose with everything in them. All around them the mountains of looming death came down, smashing, grinding the men and elephants who dared attack them. Just for a second Rockson saw through the curtains of sand about a half a mile off. There! There were the handlers of the Qu'ul devices, riding atop their camels, their hands held high, pointing the death-dealing sticks upward to hold the attacking mountains aloft. Then the dust closed again, and a boulder the size of a small truck came down just yards to the right of Rockson, sending up a mini-geyser of earth.

He was momentarily blinded, but Kral, with his extra eyelids for just such emergencies, kept barreling along behind Rahallah's massive steed. And they rode, galloped through the morning's purple haze, firing their lasers, destroying the smaller of the sky-boulders. Death smashed all around them. Humans and elephants were wiped out like so many bugs beneath a hammer, ground down into the desert sands where nothing grew and aeons of men already lay buried.

They rode and fired lasers and fought to keep back the welling tears at the devastating destruction of their own forces. All the elephants, the riders who would never see their wives or children again! The sheer hideous waste of it all! And perhaps worst of all, though they had undoubtedly gained time for the rest of the army to move out, Rockson knew one thing for certain. And it made his heart sink like a ball of lead into the ocean of his soul. There was no way in hell they were going to be able to defeat Killov even with ten thousand elephants.

CHAPTER NINETEEN

If Rockson had basically thought of himself as a man without an overabundance of fear, other than a few palpitations here and there, he was disabused of that notion as he and Rahallah rode like the wind just one step ahead of the pursuing sky-mountains. It was one thing to be killed by a man, or even taken out by one or another of the rad beasts that filled the globe. But this was of a different order. Smashed into something resembling ketchup, less than ketchup—just melted into the ground along with everything else that happened to get caught beneath the falling death.

"Come on, baby, move that big ass," Rock shouted as he leaned over toward the war bull's flapping right ear. But the great beast didn't need any prodding on that account. It was feeling its own brand of fear—an emotion that it hadn't had much experience with either. Somehow it knew that many, if not all the others, of its species who had been riding alongside it just minutes before were kaput. There was a telepathic link between the animals. And it could feel them no more. Could make no contact—just empty ether when it reached out to touch their animal souls.

The falling mountains grew even closer, smashing down on every side of them, making thundering sounds that seemed as if they would crack their very eardrums. Rock had no idea how they weren't crushed; so many of the things seemed to be landing only feet away. But though the crushing mountains were perhaps the deadliest weapon next to the atomic bomb ever invented, the handlers of the levitation stones riding far behind the damage they were causing perhaps couldn't *see* exactly what it was they were crushing. Accuracy was not at a premium. But then it didn't have to be.

They skirted along the leeward of a dune, Rahallah in the lead, his elephant ten yards ahead of Kral. On the other side of the wall of sand they could hear the immense stones stamping, searching out anything that lived. And then, luck. A thick fog bank rolled in right over the top of the desert sands. And within seconds the two elephants were lost inside, invisible to the outside world. Rahallah's elephant slowed automatically once it was a few hundred feet inside. Kral came up right behind him and grabbed his tail so they wouldn't get lost—a result of the training that the creatures had undergone over the years.

They slid off sideways through the fog, along a set of dunes. The Amun weapons-handlers didn't need to see *much* to guide their weapons—but they needed *some* sighting of targets every mile or so. As the rocks drove up and down, the two men shot away from the action. The moving mountains didn't follow, the men could hear the thunder for miles. Then the stones were heading off due southeast, toward the Nile.

Rockson leaned far forward so his chest was lying

atop the neck of the war beast. He could feel the animal below him, feel its power as the great dark legs churned through the sands like an oceanliner's propellers through the sea. They seemed to go through the thick soupy mist for an hour after the great booms had disappeared miles off. The crazy bastards under Killov's command didn't seem to have any particular strategy for conquering the countryside. Just kill everything, let the devil sort it all out later. You couldn't surrender or even agree to be on his side if he wasn't interested. Just a madman uprooting his Earth garden's human weeds with ruthless, mortal blows.

At last they emerged from the fog and could see the desert ahead for miles. Rahallah led them on, heading due south now. Rockson hadn't the foggiest idea where he was. Doubtless both elephants had more sense of location than he did right now. Which made him feel just great, in addition to the wonderful morning it had already been.

They meandered for another half hour or so through increasingly complex interwoven patterns of dunes, like a veritable maze of sand, then reached a vast and chasmed plain at the start of which the earth sank down nearly a thousand feet with sharp jutting rock formations and caves everywhere. As if he were seeing traffic signs, Rahallah just kept his beast going, threading his way right through each crevasse and chasm. Suddenly, as they rounded a bend, ten lasers were aimed at them from the trunks of ten war elephants standing side by side. Not a sight one wanted to come on unprepared! But the handlers above recognized their own and opened their ranks, staring at the two silently as it was not their rank to question.

The two men rode inside to a large grottolike

formation with stalagmites and stalactites hanging everywhere, like ice cream cones of calcium deposits. Elephants, fighters, and their wives and children were everywhere within the immense cavern, trying to set up their tents again in much more crowded circumstances. These were the ones so many were sacrificed to protect!

Rockson looked anxiously around for more of his men. Kral headed down the middle of a corridor that was kept cleared of man or beast to facilitate movement.

This was truly a nomadic army. They had pulled up stakes and were setting them back down again in the space of several hours. Homes, cooking tents, hospitals—all sprang right up, ready for function. If he had to fight alongside anybody, these seemed like the guys. Not that they or he had a chance against the Killov forces.

Rockson was relieved when he spotted Chen and Archer holding up Sheransky, one of his arms around each of them like a drunk unable to stand up on his own.

"Rock, it's Rock," Chen exclaimed, looking up with something approaching happiness on his usually stone face. "Thank the Lord you made it! We'd heard about an hour ago how the battle went— a single war elephant returned with its wounded rider. We heard that the entire diversionary force had been wiped out!"

Archer turned his head as he heard the voice and screamed out, *"Rrrroooooocck!"* with such force that a number of elephants honked back challengingly, creating quite a din—which lasted for several seconds, until their handlers told them to shut up in their own unique Egyptian/Elephant dialect.

"Yeah, we made it," Rock said. "But all the other

poor bastards with us got it. It was the worst thing I've seen in a long time, boys, and that's no lie. Wiped out in a stone-massacre. We couldn't do a goddamn thing."

Rock was frustrated, angered by the loss of so many good men and mounts. He had been especially invited over to help get this show together—but as far as he could see, it was getting worse by the second. The colonel had gotten his hands on some potent weapons indeed. And Rockson wondered, though he dared not voice the question fully even to himself, whether the bastard had at last found the very thing that might give him the entire planet delivered on a squashed silver platter.

"Rockson—we must meet with General Tutankhamen and his top staff," Rahallah shouted over to him from his elephant. "Must organize a new way to respond to the Skull's army! Please, *now!* Your men are as safe as anybody else in this blasted cave here."

"Got to go," Rock said, looking down with a good feeling that at least his own men were alive, for now. It could have been worse. "You all need anything?"

"No, we're fine, Rock. Go ahead, man," Chen said. Archer just gazed adoringly up, a few wet tears trickling out of his eyes and onto his greasy beard, as he had been *sure* Rock was dead.

Rockson turned and rode, following Rahallah's war beast. The pharaoh and his top men were already seated around on elephant footstools in a circle. Ten of them, all giving advice to Tutankhamen, who listened to each man and then told the next to have his say. Rock was glad to see there was input from the whole top staff. Democratic voicing of opinions could only open up the potential for fresh ideas.

Rock and Rahallah's mounts lowered themselves next to the other elephants of the top military leadership. With feed bags strapped on, the elephants were ready to stand there all night just chewing.

Rock jumped down on the tusk, using the quick-exit method, and was glad to find that he'd at last gotten it right. His elephant looked at him through one of those huge cup-sized eyes, gazed him up and down, and then looked away. It snorted as if to say maybe, just maybe Rockson wasn't a complete dumb-bunny after all. It still hadn't made up its mind.

Rahallah saluted the pharaoh with a three-fingers-toward-the-side-of-the-chin gesture, and Tutankhamen returned it, welcoming them both warmly.

"Your excellency," Rahallah said softly but firmly. "I must regretfully inform you that your son is dead." The pharaoh's whole face seemed to go slack for a second, and he aged about thirty years in that second. But then he pulled his grief back inside him, and his face hardened back to its typical regal demeanor filled with command.

Rock sat patiently as they all had their say. Basically, they wanted to fight, to go back and get revenge for those who were slain. They agreed that it was not for desert warriors to run like old women, not like war elephants to show their tails instead of their tusks. Then Rock and Rahallah were asked for their opinions, and the black man spoke first.

"I say your men are great fighters, among the bravest I have ever seen," Rahallah said dramatically. He had not been Premier Vassily's right hand and man-servant for decades without learning how to be the consummate politician, a suave diplomat in his own way. He had dealt with generals, leaders of countries, emperors of whole continents. Had served

174

Vassily well and learned statesmanship. He told the assembly that to counterattack without an effective new plan would be tantamount to suicide. That the weapons which he and Rock had seen in action up close were just too unstoppable with the present configuration of forces. He spoke for only a couple of minutes, but seemed to impress Tutankhamen, who looked at him, nodding his head yes almost imperceptibly. Rahallah even used an Egyptian proverb, saying that it was a foolish man who threw himself and all that he loved off the cliff, instead of finding a way down it.

Then it was Rock's turn. He didn't have to talk. There were other ways of explaining. He found a small piece of soft-stone, put it on the hard-packed cave ground, and then found a piece of broken stalagmite as big as a football. He held it up over the small stone. Then he let the stalagmite drop from about three feet. There was a quick murmuring among the assembled leaders. Rock reached down and lifted the large stone up again. Its target was smashed, broken into little pieces ready for the sandbox outside.

"You and Rahallah speak with wisdom," Tutankhamen said after there was total silence for about ten seconds. "Of course you are both right. We cannot throw ourselves beneath the rocks. But then what is our—our new course, Rockson?"

"We need a trick, a way in the backdoor, something to neutralize the damn weapons!" he exclaimed. One of the men who had been seated around the circle spoke up. Rock could see he had a sharp angular face. He looked to be eighty, perhaps ninety years old, with shrunken-in cheeks and a nose that a hawk could have loved.

"He's the power man—Sesostris—the medicine

175

man," Rahallah whispered to Rockson as the man began to speak in a slow creaking voice, as if the door of a crypt were being opened.

"I learned secrets as a child," Sesostris trembled out. "Secrets passed down from my father, who was one of the gravekeepers of the Cheops pyramids. There is a *second* level below the level where the Qu'ul sticks were found by the Cult of Amun years ago. A level containing the counter-force to the antimatter devices—the Ra sticks are the negatives of the Qu'ul that Colonel Killov is using." The man paused as if catching his breath.

"And it is said that there is a way into the pyramid that few know of. The Ra sticks exist, I know they do. The pharaohs were given the Qu'ul, it is said, by the Cat God, to build the pyramids. This must be true, for those immense slabs of rock would *not* have been lifted by mortal men. They were raised, floated over the land. All of the ancient structures were built that way! But the gods made the Ra sticks so that if mankind got out of hand with the Qu'ul, there would be something that could destroy them. These are things that I have not revealed since I heard them as a child." The shaky old man sat down heavily.

"I say, let's check out the damned things," Rockson blurted out, "before we have any more battles! We'll get a small force together and go to the pyramids. Are they far?"

"The Cheops pyramids, no. Not more than a day by elephant," Rahallah said. "I think your idea is the correct one, Rockson." Pharaoh Tutankhamen nodded in agreement.

"We can only take three men," Sesostris spoke up again. "No more can be taken inside the tomb entrance or there will be the God's wrath! Yea, the legends that speak of the Ra sticks mention only three."

Rahallah looked at Rock, and they both knew two who were going: them.

Sesostris smiled, his lips looking as if they would crack, and said, "You will need me along. Only I know the secret way inside!"

CHAPTER TWENTY

For an old man, the Egyptian witch man, Sesostris, rode his war bull like a rodeo vet out for the winning trophy. He had insisted that no one other than himself had the slightest chance of finding the passage in, or of knowing how to deal with the Ra crystals. His elephant seemed as old as he was, all wrinkled with flaps of skin hanging down everywhere. The damned thing made Rockson's own prime male bull seem like a positive teenager, and he knew Kral was at least fifty from the size of the tusks. Rahallah had told him, though, that old Sesostris and his mount could hold their own.

All three war bulls had been outfitted forward and rear in armor. The first armor layer was coverings of dried elephant hide, overlapped in opposite directions, so their opposing grains would double their strength. Over that, handmade steel mesh hung down across their chests and exposed back flanks. Often their enemies would try to stab into the great war elephants with long thin spears like icepicks eight feet long, to pierce their hearts and lungs. But now that the beasts had been wearing the armor for years, they had become more or less immune from anything other than mortars or bombs—and, of course, falling mountains.

As usual, Rock just sat back and let the big bull elephant do his thing. The animal seemed to like tearing ass, to be huffing and puffing and stamping through the sands like the Pony Express. He was in his element out here in the midst of the desolation. Like Rockson. And suddenly Rock realized with a mad kind of enlightenment that he and the war bull were probably more alike than he could imagine. Too alike.

There was a mist-streaked sky on that night of adventure, with stars peeking through here and there from above, not giving a whole lot of light for travel. With the moon in hibernation the desert was dark, a long flat highway of smooth impenetrable blackness, as if one would just fall off into nothingness where they went. But Sesostris beelined in one direction, and they kept on behind him, following his mount's pale blue guide-light.

They went over smooth fields of sand miles long, then rolling slopes like waves across a pond. At last, after about six hours of riding hard with only two quick oasis rest stops—for the elephants to water—they came to a very high dune. They climbed to its summit and, as they started down, Rockson could see—just barely—a series of tall obelisks set hundreds of feet apart, forming a monumental roadway to the Great Pyramid of Cheops. And that great pyramid stood perhaps a mile ahead of them, the most majestic silhouette against the stars Rock had ever seen. In the center of the giant columns, Cheops towered a good 500 feet into the air.

They stood there, silently taking in its grandeur, lingering as the new day's sun began lightening the sky to the east—a violet, rippling color. Rockson felt

179

his breath quicken. The place was overwhelming, built on a scale as if the gods themselves were coming down to live and die there. Cheops looked so ancient, so eroded by time, yet so strong, still withstanding the elements which were ceaseless.

Sesostris mumbled aloud, as if he were remembering things. Rock hoped he was remembering entrances, passages he had forgotten since being a child so many years ago.

The Southern Egyptians had taken it all over nearly sixty years before, and he'd had to flee with his father to the Northern Army, where he had friends. It had been a long, long time, but now he was back.

At last the wizened witch man turned his war bull around and led them down the dune to what looked like a wall of dark sand nearby. Sesostris had them get their elephants to use their tusks and trunks to dig through the stuff for about ten minutes. Suddenly an opening appeared—and inside they could see a stone door, elaborately carved.

"Yes, still here," Sesostris said. "My childhood memories do not deceive me." He spoke with terrible solemnity. Rock expected an exultant smile. Not so. He just stared out at the world as if he knew too many nasty secrets about the great mysteries of life to smile anymore. "We go in through here. The tunnel leads the way beneath the dunes, and over to the pyramid. We'd never get through the guards around there." He had his elephant reach out with its massive trunk, the laser beam retracted inside for the moment, and wrap it around an immense circular brass handle that looked as bright as the day it had been put on. The black sand of Cheops had kept the whole thing preserved in mint condition for four thousand years. The immense stone doors, each one a single block the size of a truck, swung open on perfect stone-ball bearings situated beneath them.

Sesostris led his elephant in on foot, since the rock ceiling was too low to ride beneath. Even then the great beasts had to half kneel down as they made their way through the carved stone entrance into the square tunnel ahead. Rock jumped down, and Rahallah followed suit. Each walked a yard in front of their war beasts, which followed on their tethers, looking around nervously. War elephants didn't like being cooped up on every side. Their sheer size made them wary of getting stuck in anything smaller than a valley.

The air smelled dank, filled with death. Why not? Whatever was in here had been rotting and mildewed for aeons. The place was cold too, bizarrely cold considering that it had stood in the sun for so damned long. You could have preserved meats inside there. They had to move very slowly through the narrowing tunnel, the war bulls getting increasingly nervous.

Suddenly, they were through into a larger chamber a good hundred feet on a side, a perfect square with high ceilings and small obelisks standing ten feet apart all along the walls. The floor here was stone as well, big squares cut into ten-by-ten-foot pieces and then set alongside one another with perfect fit. A virtually flawless juncture of joints. Whoever had built all this sure knew what they were doing, and used tools unknown to modern man.

Suddenly it dawned on Rock that he was seeing—without sunlight, without torches! How was it possible? He glanced around, and realized that it was the walls themselves; they were emitting a very faint greenish blue light that appeared almost like early twilight to the eye. It was phosphorescent, like the water beneath the surface of a swamp, which can

181

glow with the microscopic life below. But this glow was buried in the rock. It seemed to emanate from deep within, as if something had grown in the very walls.

It gave enough light even after thousands of years so they could clearly make out the major details of the place. And he could feel that the longer he was down there, the more his eyes were adjusting, allowing the dim light in. Shecter would have given his right frontal lobe to see some of this stuff! Rock hesitated for a second, thinking to scrape a little off one of the walls. Then thought better of it.

"We leave the war bulls here," Sesostris said.

CHAPTER TWENTY-ONE

Rock and Rahallah followed the witch man down one of a dozen smaller tunnel systems which snaked out from every side of the vast stone chamber. Here the greenish light was a little dimmer, but because it was narrower they could see well enough. It was strange, seeing by the low and evened-out glow that came from the very rock walls. What secrets was the wizard priest leading them to? Rockson wondered if Sesostris really knew this place. Especially how to get back out.

The tunnel grew narrower and narrower, until it was shrunken down to perhaps four feet high and not more than thirty-six inches wide. Talk about feeling like you were walking in a sardine can! Rahallah had it the hardest, being in the six-ten range. He ended up almost crawling along, smashing his shoulders, head, and knees into outcroppings of stone ornamentation which were everywhere in the tunnel. They moved in deeper, heading at a steeply downward angle. The air just grew thicker and thicker now, more like dust than air, as if the very oxygen were petrified. Rock let out a few violent sneezes, and Sesostris looked around angrily, as if it wasn't the greatest idea. Then, with no warning, they turned a corner and were into another chamber, this one's green light brighter than the others by far. Bright as a shopping mall by comparison. Rockson could see every part of the chamber.

And he could hardly believe his eyes: mummies, golden coffins, statues of lions, of serpents, and of giant scarab beetles forged out of gold and silver. Rock knew all the treasures of all the museums of the twentieth century hadn't contained the glitter and wealth that lay before their mesmerized eyes. It was a veritable warehouse of the stuff.

"What—what—is all this?" Rockson asked hesitantly as they stood side by side just inside the tunnel, staring out over the nearly ten-acre underground site.

"It is the resting place of the really great pharaohs," Sesostris answered, making a circular motion over his heart several times. His craggy face was even more sucked in, and Rockson knew he could feel the gods within this place, gods both good and evil. Rockson could too. The past was everywhere, the ghosts of the ancient dead darting along the walls, among the massive columns. The caskets were bigger and more bejeweled than any Chicago gangster's hearse could ever be. They *knew* how to die back then!

"Your Colonel Killov has taken the Qu'ul powersticks from the level that is above this one," Sesostris said. He looked straight up. "Maybe two hundred feet above, far too thick a layer of stone for us to be found out wandering down here. This chamber is older than that which was thought to be the oldest by Egyptologists and historians. This was built at least a thousand years before the First Dynasty. Built when men were giants and hundred-foot serpents still roamed the earth. Egypt is the most ancient civilization, gentlemen." He sighed reverentially, scan-

184

ning back and forth what was the resting place of those who had lived back then. "The beginning of recorded history dates back to 4241 B.C., when our ancient ancestors created the first calendar. Tukyur, the Yellow Kingdom, had existed for a thousand years before that. And the Scarab Worshippers perhaps another thousand years before that. There is no culture more ancient than ours. None more connected to the secret mysteries of the beginning. These creatures," he said, pointing around at the sculptures made out of gold and onyx, out of pure blue crystal rocks ten feet high, out of substances not known on the earth today, "these lions with wings, jackals with human heads, the great scarabs which kept men as slaves, were once real. These are not myths—they are facts. This is how it truly once was in the very dawn of man's history. These statues depict real beings!"

Rockson didn't need a hell of a lot of convincing about any of it. The mummy cases themselves seemed huge, nearly twelve feet long, far bigger than what he remembered from the spooky ruined museum he had visited in Denver when he was a child, when his father had taken him. Parts of it were still there, untouched. It had been a powerful experience, but he hadn't seen anything like this! The carvings of solid gold, of horned and winged creatures which hung suspended on chains in various parts of the granite block ceiling seemed almost real, as if they might move at any moment. The detail and size of everything was absolutely astounding. Rock knew that in the old days any one of these pieces would have been worth millions of dollars.

"There—that is what we came for," the wizard said as he suddenly spotted the object of their journey sitting dead center in the room, in what looked like a glass bowl atop a golden-legged lion-pawed table. "The Gizeh Jar—and inside it the three Ra sticks! These are what was used to create the great pyramids, to lift their huge stones!

Rockson and Rahallah both sighted the objects sitting about a hundred and fifty feet away, surrounded by what looked like twelve or so upright golden caskets with huge faces sculpted onto them, jeweled eyes staring out.

The glowing green/blue sticks that sat upright in a bowl of clear crystals seemed to almost waver in the air, their appearance becoming sometimes indistinct, as if they were fading away into another dimension—and then with sharp little crackling sounds become fully visible again. They were filled with an electrical life-source that touched back to the birth of the planet, back to when forces beyond modern man's ken were at work. Rockson felt himself hypnotized by the items, wanting to reach for them, walk toward them, possess the Ra sticks!

"No, do not move!" Sesostris shouted. "Approach them wrongly, and you will die! Don't even look directly at them!"

CHAPTER TWENTY-TWO

The three men of the 21st century stood looking at the glowing Ra sticks of the year 6278 B.C. On a golden table nearby, Sesostris found gloves that looked as if they were woven from gold. They were shining and flawless. "These have to be put on to handle the Ra sticks," Sesostris explained.

Rock only looked out of the corner of his eye at the iridescent tubes, remembering the wizard's warnings. The three crystal tubes of incalculable power were standing up on end, one against the other, on one side of the crystal container. They called out for him to reach for them, to hold them. But he found it easier to resist now that he wasn't looking straight at them; the hypnotic strength was far less. Gingerly, they approached the sticks.

"The Ra sticks draw all men," Sesostris said in awe, squinting down at the things from different angles as if trying to absorb their godly powers without actually gazing on the face of god. "These were designed to draw your soul. Only those pure of heart can resist. Those with base desires for the Ra— would touch. Or try to. And die a most horrible death, for they can't be taken out of the crystal container, unless in direct proximity to their opposites, their antitheses on a molecular level—the Qu'ul sticks! Then the Ra sticks will direct their energy toward the Qu'ul. And the two combine and annihilate one another. It is better that the world not have any such things. They are the tools of the ancients. Mankind has done enough damage, using them as weapons!''

"Amen to that," Rock said, having no desire to take any of these super-weapons back to the U.S. of A. Like the man said, humankind wasn't ready. It hadn't risen much above the ape stage as far as he could see. "But—what about Killov's Qu'ul sticks?''

"Now, we must take these and try to carry out a mission of total destruction of the Qu'ul sticks, Rockson," Sesostris intoned. "Even if we die saving the planet Earth, the gods and demons, the netherworlds themselves would honor us. Such an honor has not been bestown on any mortal man since time immemorial!''

With the rippling gold-seamed gloves on his hands, the high priest reached forward and grasped hold of the crystal jar containing the Ra sticks. Rockson watched the gloved hands close around it incredibly slowly and carefully. The container, which was vase shaped but with subtle in-and-out curvations, was made of some kind of crystal that was seamed with networks of veins of a more shimmering ultra-blue. The whole thing looked somehow alive, as if it had to pump energy through those veins to withstand the pulsing green sticks inside, to contain them.

Rahallah and Rockson both held their breaths as Sesostris lifted, and the crystal container rose free of the table with a slight popping sound, as if a small vacuum had been broken after many thousand years. They had both half expected the universe to explode or a genie to appear—but nothing happened at all.

Sesostris held the thing as if cradling a child, and started walking slowly, retracing his steps back through the mummies, masks, and monster-memorabilia of a long-gone era.

"We must go slow," the priest said. "It cannot be covered in any way, must always be allowed to 'breathe.' You two will protect me. We must reach Killov's storage place for the Qu'ul."

"We're with you, pal, all the way," Rock said, trying to give encouragement to the man. What pressure he was under! The mental pressure of not dropping the only goddamned thing that could save the world was too damned much!

Naturally, they got lost! The high priest gave up on trying to find the elephants, and instead took a steep staircase. To a dead end!

"We are out," the wizard man said triumphantly as he strode onto the top landing.

Rock didn't see any exit door! But the wizened priest moved forward a few yards, holding the Ra jar out toward the wall, as if he was offering it some food. Then the whole thing seemed to pop out of its slot, and daylight flooded in. The stone that had fallen out to the sand was a good eight feet in diameter, and they stepped through easily and out onto the desert. They were right at the base of the great pyramid.

"Now we must make our way back to the war bulls—and—" But Sesostris's mouth couldn't even finish the sentence, for suddenly there were nets being dropped over them, steel-mesh woven cables that completely entangled Rockson and Rahallah before they could move a muscle. They fell to the ground and looked on in horror through the metal web at Colonel Killov. The KGB nemesis was clad in a bizarre, overdone jewel-and-feather outfit. He walked up to Sesostris.

"Give it to me," he said, holding out both of his boney hands, his eyes lit with a drug-fueled fire. "Give it to me, my priestly friend." Killov grinned, so his face looked truly skull-like. Even the high priest, who had seen much of death in his day, shuddered at this face.

"No, never," Sesostris said firmly, holding onto the thing. "Besides, if you take this from me now, before it's been united with the Qu'ul, we'll all go up in fire."

"That's where you're wrong," Killov replied. "I have a way of controlling the power of the Ra sticks. As for you—your life means nothing to me. I have searched for a year to find those Ra sticks. Now that you have brought them to me, I will be invincible! Kill him!"

Two men suddenly rushed forward before the aged priest could move an inch to defend himself. Two long narrow swords went through his armoring from each side of the restraining net, straight into his chest. He gasped out, "No!" He was having trouble breathing, and Killov reached out and suddenly grabbed the crystal jar through an opening in the net, before the dying man could stop him. Sesostris threw his arms around his chest as if he was trying to hold it in, and then his head snapped back and a gush of bright red blood came cascading out of his

190

open mouth.

When the two robed attackers pulled their swords back out, the blades were followed by two fountains of red.

Sesostris toppled backwards into the sand, staining it a purplish color which faded fast as the thirsty desert drank down all that he offered.

"You sick bastards," Rockson screamed from his netting trap. "That man was a high priest to thousands of people, a holy man."

"Sick? Yes." Killov laughed as he looked down at his squirming prisoners. "But stupid, no." He nodded, and two men rushed over with a dark blanket of some kind. The weaving was made of a super-fine material, almost like a spider's web. Killov placed the crystal inside the black material, closed it around the crystal container, and then tied it at the top with a knot of the same material that was braided together into a thicker twine.

"The net of precious Kanth webs." Killov grinned down at Rockson. It made him feel so good just to have captured the man he hated above all others on the face of the earth. But to see him witness this total humiliation and defeat on his part was an unparalleled thrill! All the pain and suffering that Killov had endured for the last few years, all of it suddenly seemed worth it!

"It's controlled once inside the Kanth web," the colonel said, wanting Rockson to understand just how clever the KGB ruler could be. "Modern technology actually, not ancient. It's a coil of superconducting wires made of plastic. When a current is sent through the web it creates a field which nothing can penetrate. Nothing can get through the tangled flow of currents. The Ra sticks are blind in there. Blind as a man with both his eyes plucked out. And they are at my disposal. Thank you for this wonderful new weapon! You see, if these Ra sticks can neutralize the Qu'ul, there has got to be a way they can enhance them too! My scientists will soon discover how.''

CHAPTER TWENTY-THREE

The nets were gathered up, and Rockson and Rahallah were carried atop Killov's Nubian slaves' backs like animals. They were put up on camels, huge mutant beasts about half again as big as Rock had remembered camels to be. They had three humps, creating a double row of seats up there between them. Rockson was thrown up top unceremoniously like a bag of potatoes, his hands tied behind his back. He was squeezed by the humps of a truly wretched-smelling animal, with his face pressed right into the hairy sand-gritted hide. Rahallah was thrown on the camel next to Rock's. Sesostris was left there, lying stone-cold dead in the sand, his royal blood tinting the desert in a ring around his body, oozing slowly out in every direction.

"Thanks for trying, pal," Rockson muttered down as his camel walked past the outstretched priest, somehow serene in his demise. That was all that you could ever do—try. Fate did the rest. Rahallah, too, uttered a few of his own witch-doctor prayers as he passed behind on the next camel in the convoy of eight. They rode for a good two hours, Killov in the lead, sitting up there with one of the red Qu'ul power sticks ready to lift up and smash anything that took his fancy. As the convoy made its way along the desert, Killov popped whole handfuls of pills into his thin lips, so pleased was he with his recent successes. And once he got a nice buzz on, and was feeling really mellow, he began using his Qu'ul, ripping up thorn trees, dunes, even animals running along the sands, and playing with them. He'd lift things up, then he would stop the power beam, suddenly making them drop from hundreds of feet up. A smile crossed his face each time the object of his affections smashed to the ground and was destroyed.

Rock's stomach and chest were taking a pounding up on the camel's back. It could move pretty good through the sand, but it wasn't what you would call a smooth ride. It made the war elephants feel like they had Rolls-Royce suspension systems.

It took them three hours of solid riding to reach a whole series of small pyramids with an immense one that seemed to reach for the sky in the center: the Great Pyramid of Gizeh. Killov's headquarters.

It was clearly the KGB lunatic's homebase, for guards were everywhere, armed with conventional rifles and machine guns. Black-uniformed elite guards, each with one of the Qu'ul sticks, stood at each of the sides of the pyramid, in emplacements high up that had been carved out of the very side of the pyramid. Killov was not what you would call a strong believer in landmarks or preserving the past. Just rip down the Sphinx, renovate the pyramids. No problem! On the other hand, Rockson remembered, if his history was correct, that McDonald's had—just before the Nuke War—set up a burger joint right inside Grant's Tomb. The McGrant—if he remembered the name correctly from the *American Culture of the Past* book he had once read—was sold there.

But Rockson had more things to worry about than the lack of good hamburger joints in the late 2090's. A huge slab of rock at the base of the pyramid opened, and the whole crew rode in on the camels. The doorway had been cut out a good twenty feet high. They didn't mess around out here, Rockson had to give them that. But with those anti-grav sticks that Killov had managed to get his bloody hands on, you could think big. Remembering how much effort he and others had put into working on Century City's tunnels, strengthening those that fell down, building new ones—a few devices like this would save the city incredible amounts of time and energy. It could mean almost a Renaissance for CC—more time for studies and meditation, rehabilitating some of the nearby wastelands. Time spent on developing things useful to man, not manhandling rocks.

Inside, the camels kneeled down, and Rock and Rahallah were each removed by several men from their respective mounts. They were carried down a tunnel with wall friezes of lions holding swords in all four paws and slicing off human heads, which were depicted falling to the earth in piles. Yeah, this must be the right place, Rockson mused sullenly as they were carried past the torches that were placed up on walls every fifty feet or so in ornate golden holders. The torches lit the procession with flickering bands of light and shadow.

They were carried into a religious assembly chamber with huge carvings of dogs and hawks, the place where Killov led the priests of Amun in their daily rituals, keeping firm control over them all. Two wide stone tables coated in purplish dried slime were in the center of the circular room, which was forty feet in diameter. An arched ceiling rose up some thirty feet above.

Rockson and Rahallah were carried to the slime-tables, and then tied down. Killov wouldn't take the slightest chance with these two. He, above all men, knew the power of each one. He knew that it was incredible luck that he had been able to capture both of them. The dark gods were clearly winning in the battle with the gods of light. And his own dark plans were being favored at an accelerated pace.

Once the two were securely bound with steel wire to bronze ringlets embedded within the great sacrificial stones, Killov had his men cut the netting still encasing them apart with steel clippers.

They struggled violently once it was cut, testing the metal binds that held them down. But they were unbreakable.

"Yes, try to break it." Killov chuckled as he stood at one end of Rockson's slab. "It gives me such pleasure to see you struggling like this. Like animals caught in a trap. And soon I shall hear you scream as well. Music for my ears. In fact, I shall have the whole event recorded, video and audio, so I can have a permanent record of the torture and death of Ted Rockson and Premier Vassily's black lackey. Ah, here it is now," the KGB madman said as men brought video equipment in on their backs and set up two cameras with stereo mikes at each end of the two sacrificial altars. Within minutes the equipment was turned on, torches placed in stone holders around the room so it was lit up with a flaring brilliance.

"Now, Rockson," Killov said, getting Rock's attention. He had been looking around, trying to see if there was any way in hell to get free. The dozen priests, with gold vestments over their shoulders and long, dark red robes hanging to the hard floor, looked at him with infinite coldness and not a trace of mercy. "There's nothing I want from you other than to see you die. No information, nothing. So there's nothing you can do to stop me—no enticements. And all that will add to my pleasure. For you to know there's no way out." He hefted a glowing red Qu'ul in his hand, and pointed it at one of several slabs resting on their sides against one wall. The piece rose right up as light as a feather and started drifting across the room until it was hovering over Rockson.

Rock looked up and gulped. It was the exact size of the slab he was on, about six by ten feet. And looked to be about six feet thick. That meant when the bastard slammed it down on him, it would squash him into bug juice.

"I'm sure you're thinking I'm going to crush you. But I'm not, I'm not." Killov laughed, his drug-hazed eyes floating around in the narrow cavernous face like eggs in an overgreased frying pan. "Well, at least not right away. You know what amazes me most about these Qu'ul anti-gravity devices?" Killov went on. Rockson was unable to take his eyes away from the floating tons just six feet above him. "Their precision!"

"Courage, friend, courage," Rahallah whispered over from his slab several yards away. "The gods will look highly upon you." Even as he spoke, one of the Amun priests appeared at the end of his table, and using a second Qu'ul power-stick, lifted a piece of rock as big as, if not bigger than, Rockson's. In a flash it was over Rahallah's body, hanging there like a blimp ready to run out of gas.

"Yes, I'm sure the gods will welcome you, won't they?" Killov laughed sharply like a hysterical woman. "And they'll have you soon. But not so easily—or in one piece. As I was saying, Rockson, what amazes me most about these Qu'ul is the precision with which one can operate them once you

197

become adept. As I have. They're like scalpels. They can be focused in so many ways. For example, although that is at least ten tons of rock above you, I can lower it at a very slow speed." He started bringing it down but fractions of an inch at a time.

"Or," Killov suddenly spat out with a shrill madness, "I can move it fast." Suddenly the slab was dropping right on him, coming down like a meteor from hell. It loomed huge within hundredths of a second, and Rock's eyes snapped shut involuntarily, not wanting to see the end. But then another second passed, and another. And Rock knew there was no way in hell it would take more than two seconds for that slab to fall the last inch onto his flesh. He snapped his eyes open, and was looking up at the slab, micrometers from his nose.

"And then you can stop it again, anywhere. Isn't it amazing?" Killov exclaimed. "I'm going to crush you, Rockson, slowly. Very slowly. You will feel every bone in your body snap, shall feel the very cells of your flesh exploded before I am done with you. Feel your eyeballs pop from your head like rotten fruits." Killov turned his hand just slightly, the red beam cloaking the entire slab with a crackling, almost invisible sheen of red electricity starting to move again.

Rock could feel it coming down agonizingly slowly. He turned his head sideways, and had to pull in his chest. He winced. It hurt already as it squashed his ear against the side of his skull. And then the skull began compressing slightly as the death slab dropped down another twentieth of an inch in a minute.

Killov was right. Rockson could see that already. This death was going to hurt a lot.

CHAPTER TWENTY-FOUR

As the six-ton slab inched its way down, the pressure in Rockson's skull was unbearable, as if his brains were trying to come out of him and escape. As if the whole damn show might explode out of his ears, eyes, nose, and mouth at any second. His chest was also being pushed down so that he could only take extremely shallow breaths, each one less than the next—all of which only added to his panic.

He wasn't exactly afraid of death, as he had been around it too long. He knew that it was going to come knocking on his door some day. He was not even afraid of dying. But he did feel fear of this inhuman monstrosity crushing him down into Freefighter marmalade. A death that was very, very messy.

The pain was unbearable—something of a new order for Rockson, who had experienced the gamut of unpleasurable sensations. A few pleasurable ones as well. But this was a new piece in the cosmic jigsaw puzzle of pain. One piece he would have just as gladly done without.

Rock could hear Killov's cackling, and then the sound of his own chest bones and the side of his head starting to make a very faint crunching sound. Snap-crackle-pop time wasn't very far away. Then, even as he waited to start cracking like Humpty Dumpty up on the sacrificial wall, the slab stopped in its tracks. His right ear felt about as flat as a piece of American cheese. He winced in pain and waited for Killov to continue his fun and games—after prolonging the torture another few seconds—to get on with the show. Then Rockson thought he heard a commotion of some kind even above the slamming sounds of his own heart pounding in his ears like a kettle drum.

Yes, definitely, someone was talking. Rock somehow managed to turn his eyes all the way down toward the bottom of the narrow space, and looked between the slab he was lying on and the one that was pressing down from above. A black-garbed figure had his hand around the front of Killov's throat. What looked like—from Rockson's vantage point, though he couldn't be sure—a long, nasty-looking blade was pressed up hard against that throat.

"Now, you're going to raise that slab up, Colonel," the voice demanded firmly, saying each word clearly so Killov and all fifteen or so assorted guards and priests standing around the ritual sacrifice room got the message. "And no one here wants to try anything—or there's one dead KGB slime, and I mean pronto. I'll slice his throat from eye to eye if one of you makes the slightest move. You—priesty," the black-cloaked figure yelled to the priest who controlled Rahallah's death slab and had it down pushing into him about as much as Rockson's. "*Move it!*" the figure shouted again, and pulled the blade tighter against Killov's neck so that a thin line of blood appeared where it was touching.

The colonel's eyes were popping, wide as hundred-ruble pieces as he held the Qu'ul out in his hand,

trying not to make it jerk or waver as he suddenly realized that his life depended on the state of Rockson's health. His hand suddenly shook slightly from side to side as a fear-induced drug tremor swept along his arm. Rockson felt the immense slab slide back and forth over him like the biggest piece of sandpaper that had ever existed. It didn't push down any further, but it scraped over him, rubbing the side of his head. And a whole area of scalp was stone-ground off from a four-inch area.

But then—it was rising. Rock could hardly dare believe it. He was sure he'd bought it this time. He'd already been preparing for how he'd present himself to God. But the slab kept rising up above him, like a balloon, climbing easily into the air—the most beautiful sight he'd ever seen. When it was about six feet up, the black-clad figure turned Killov, forcing him to turn to the side, so that the whole slab moved as well.

"Now put it down, Colonel—and you live—I swear," the mysterious black-clad figure standing behind Killov said with icy command. The colonel somehow believed the words. He could tell if men were lying. It was one of his abilities, his secret tricks. Such a skill had enabled him to take out threats to his power long before they had a chance to strike. Preemptive termination was his rule. But not this time.

The immense slab came down fast. It hit the ground about twenty feet away with a great smash, making the whole chamber shake and some grains of sand fall from the stone ceiling over the assemblage. A roll of thunder went echoing back and forth between the walls of the place.

Just as the second stone, the one raised over Rahallah, came down next to the first, and the floor

trembled slightly again, Killov suddenly threw up his arms, grabbing the knife with both hands. He ripped the knife away from his neck, pulled it down hard, cutting his left hand severely. But Killov managed to suddenly duck down and rush through the dusty sacrifice chamber.

Like a rat he disappeared behind a low stone sculpture, and in the flash of an eye was gone.

"Son of a bitch!" the cloaked figure croaked out, throwing back his covering hood. It was Chen. Rock stared in astonishment, his mouth hanging open as the ninja-suited martial master came running the few yards up to Rock in quick sliding steps, as if he was on ice.

"No time," Chen hissed out. "I will use Quick-charge!" Rockson knew the substance Chen was referring to—a compact, high-powered explosive that was used by crews at CC for doing tunnel work. Chen must have taken some from his star-knives.

Rockson turned his head as Chen raced around the ritual slab slapping little pieces of what looked like bubblegum on the four half-inch-thick ringlets that held his wrists and ankles. The ringlets were locked somehow, and they were anchored right into the rock itself, so they had to be blasted.

Even as Chen rounded the head of the sacrificial altar and rushed toward Rahallah's table, three of the priests pulled long straight swords from beneath their priestly garb and started toward him, to cut him off. Without missing a beat, the Chinese martial-arts master whipped out three of his patented explosive shurikens. They were five-pointed kill-stars filled with the same basic kind of material as the charges on Rock's bindings.

The three starknives spun through the air, making

a slight whistling noise. They made contact faster than a man could pull a pistol and fire. The shuriken slammed into three red-robed chests, which instantly exploded out into a haze of blood and shattered bone. The three devil-priests flew backward, not even able to scream—they just gurgled loudly.

Chen raced around Rahallah's table as well, slapping the Quickcharge in place. He was at the third ringlet when Rock's mini-charges went off. There were four sharp pops and little puffs of black smoke. The charges were extremely small and made to fire tremendous force basically in one direction.

Rockson sat up fast, rubbing his definitely warmed-up ankles and wrists. They were numb from the proximity of the contained explosions. Not that he was complaining. He had barely gotten himself swung around on the table when two more of Killov's priests rushed at him, stabbing out with their long daggerlike swords. Rockson threw himself backward straight over the table as the swords dug into the stone just where his back had been a second before. He rolled off the other side without stopping, and came down standing.

He had just hit the ground when Rahallah's charges went off behind him. The black man was up in a flash and rolled off the table to be next to Rockson. Chen joined them, leaping over the table like a black gazelle.

"You crazy bastard," Rock said, looking at Chen with a dumb smile pasted all over his face. "How the hell did—"

"Later, Rock," Chen said, handing them each a fully loaded 25-shot Liberator 9-mm autopistol he produced from under the black silk ninja gear. Their weapons had been confiscated by the priests when

they had been netted. Rockson swore the guy could pull out half the weapons known to man from under that black suit of his. Chen raised his head fast from behind the table where the three of them were crouched as a few more sand-devils made their move. He let loose with four of the shurikens.

These didn't explode. They didn't have to. They just dug into faces, shoulders, and necks. And bit in hard. Four more would-be killers went staggering around, blood gushing out like cherub-fountains on a rich man's lawn.

"Killov's already out of here," Chen said as he dropped back down again. "We gotta move. I think he'll take out this whole pyramid if he has to—to get us. I'm sure he has it set with charges! I'll take the lead."

"Move," Rock said, resting his hand on the man's shoulder for an instant. "Thanks," he added. But it was too late. Chen was already up and right over the top of the closest slab-table like a panther on the run. Rock and Rahallah followed right behind so the three of them formed a sort of phalanx. They smashed out with punches and elbows and let loose with their respective weapons, taking out anything that moved toward them. And a lot did move as the whole room became a tornado of flashing swords and a few glowing red Qu'ul sticks as the priests tried to get a bead on the swift-weaving bodies.

Suddenly Chen was rising up in the air, enveloped in the sparkling red electromagnetic beam from the Qu'ul. Within an instant he was up twenty feet, heading to a smashing visit to the stone-arch ceiling. But Rock got a bead on the anti-grav-tube manipulator and sliced a seam of 9-mm slugs from neck to bellybutton. The priest went flying backward, the red glowing power-stick dropping from

his hand.

Chen dropped straight down. For most men a twenty-foot fall would have meant rather serious injury, broken bones at the least. But the Chinese Freefighter dropped like a cat, spinning around in the air so he came down feet first. He landed in a crouch on both feet, letting his whole body go down almost to the floor with the motion, knees bending.

Then he was up alongside them again in a flash, not even fazed by the air ride, ripping two more of the shuriken out from under his black garb, one in each hand. He charged out of the room through an arched doorway that led to tunnels.

A single guard tried to chop down at Rahallah with his broad sword, but the African prince grabbed him off balance and threw the man halfway across the room, smashing him into a stone wall. He wasn't in the mood to be trifled with today.

Chen led them at full run down the tunnel. They could hear noises all around them, men running down other tunnel systems. They tore ass as if there was no tomorrow. A group of five Amun guards charged out of one of the side tunnels, screaming like banshees as they came with scimitar-swords descending. Rock fired a burst of 9-mm fury, and the shots went into the first two in the pack, sending them crashing into their pals behind them. The whole crew collapsed in confusion, cutting one another. Yet still more came.

The escapees shot up an angled walkway, and then suddenly could see sunlight ahead. The tunnel narrowed, and they were at a triangular window about three feet on each side. Chen fit through first, and they saw him disappear downward. Rock went next, diving through in a hail of old-fashioned hot lead. The black warrior was right behind. Below,

about eight feet down, was a war elephant with Chen sitting on its neck. Rock landed on both feet on the bull's back. It didn't even feel it. He jumped into the battle platform—a low one with weapons tied down all over it.

Then Rahallah came down on his feet on the back part of the papyrus platform, causing some damage —but what the hell, who cared?

Chen yelled at the war beast to move tail. *"Qul aktar!"* he screamed out, the command for full cruising speed.

The bull took off like a racehorse on steroids. Its huge legs pumped wildly as it went off over the sand and straight away from the giant pyramid. And not a moment too soon. Dozens of guards appeared on the pyramid's second and third levels and began firing at them. Bullets whizzed all around them, a few slamming into the light armor of the animal, which stopped the shots from entering even the outer edge of the thick hide.

Then from the higher sections, two Qu'ul-wielders who had a view of the fleeing prisoners began sending out their red levitation beams. Wherever they struck, whole craters suddenly appeared as the desert particles were sucked up in multi-ton loads, and then slammed down again toward the elephant.

But this bull had been trained to dodge and run, never head in a straight line when attacking or being attacked. The elephant moved fast, but all over the place, turning crazy circles, moving straight ahead for a hundred yards, then suddenly lurching at a right angle to its path.

From the pyramids, as the Amun troops tried to get a bead on the thing, it looked as if it were drunk or something, moving around like that. Which made it almost impossible to get a good sighting. At the

speed it was moving the nuke-mutated elephant bull was a half mile away from the pyramid within the first sixty-five seconds. A full mile in another eighty seconds. Even the Qu'ul power sticks lost their range after a thousand yards.

"The Ra crystals! We've got to get them," Rock screamed out through the whirling sand which stormed around them. The whole desert was alive with the exploding craters of the anti-grav attempts to take them out.

"They are the counter-force to the Qu'ul!"

"Killov has hidden them!" Chen yelled. "I saw his men take a shroud-wrapped thing off. I can guess its new location." Chen, half turning his head as the war bull charged on, added, "Maybe we shouldn't go there now. I mean, just look behind you!"

Rockson turned, as did Rahallah, both men kneeling down in the thickly matted papyrus platform, holding the leather hand-grips. It looked as if an army was pouring out of the main pyramid, and the smaller ones around it as well. Chen exhorted the beast to give it everything it had inside. More than it had ever given before. *"Cha-qul-aktar-shrul!"* ("Move, or you're a McPachyderm!")

"Shit," Rock snorted as he watched the rays light the sky, watched the first great slabs of stone start rising up into the air and coming down with that dreaded thump less than a mile behind them.

From the numbers that were gathering—thousands of rushing ants, from where Rockson was sitting—it looked as if the whole damned population of Africa was getting ready to come after them.

207

CHAPTER TWENTY-FIVE

The three Freefighters bounced on just ahead of the smash-stones! Afternoon turned to dusk, and night fell with the speed of an executioner's descending sword. Chen had busted their asses out of Killov's bone-smashing hellhole, but none of them had any illusions that they were more than a cat's whisker away from pulpy termination. They could hear the constant pounding thumps of huge rocks levitated and then dropped behind them. It was like a herd of pile drivers smashing violently up and down.

Colonel Killov was surely leading them now, and was pulling out all the punches. K-Day. There was no question about it. For behind them, the entire Amun Army was forming into its combat units: cavalry of camels, cultist infantry right behind it—and of course, up front, Killov and his cadre of priests carrying the Qu'ul power-sticks. "Squash everything" was the motto of the day.

When Chen stopped the war bull on a particularly high dune, they could see through the night-binoculars that a virtual wall of camels and men was filling up the long horizon, just visible in the

starlight and the light from the crescent moon hanging like a guillotine in the velvet sky. Killov's force moved, but even their fastest camels couldn't keep up with a Class A war bull in his prime.

The escapees rushed on through the endless miles of sand for two hours. Then ahead Rock suddenly saw the great Nile flowing by, stretching a good mile across. The air was filled with precious moisture, which made the war bull honk a few times with its eight-foot trunk. It wanted to drink after exerting so much energy, after building up so much heat from its pumping muscles. It tore right through a grove of low palm trees, not looking particularly hard where it was going, snapping dozens of them right over like toothpicks. Even as Chen tried to guide it to the right to start heading south, the bull kept on with its own will, straight for the river.

"I think we're going to—" Chen just had time to say when the elephant reached the bank—a drop of about two feet—and leaped out like the biggest fat man that had ever jumped from a diving board into a swimming pool looking for heat relief. It hit the water with a tremendous splash, and then began a wild flurry of honking and shaking. It covered itself with the wet muddy stuff, whipping up its trunk filled with water and spraying it out. The three Freefighters hung on, not sure what the hell was happening. The bull doused itself and the men with trunkfuls of the cooling river water, and drank from it as well with loud slurping and gulping sounds. All in all, it put on quite a dramatic performance.

"What the hell is he doing?" Rock screamed out as the papyrus platform filled with a foot of water. Rock, Chen, and Rahallah were in a wading pool.

"I think it's the elephant's method of cooling off."

Rahallah laughed. "Otherwise he'd just blow out his whole system from the heat generated by all this running. He knows what he's doing better than we do." And Rahallah's observation was correct, for after not more than three minutes, the elephant emerged from the water dripping wet. It seemed to be ready to carry out further commands as it stood there dripping, almost motionless, letting the slight wind sweep over its huge body as the water evaporated, creating a cooling effect. An organic air conditioner.

Rockson heard the smash-stones again. Catching up. "Okay, let's head downriver and lose them—and find our own army!" Chen said, patting the beast on the back of its head. It raised its great skull up and down as if nodding yes. Rockson couldn't help but continue to hope they would find some refuge at the end of this wild ride. A lifelong elephant-rider no doubt wouldn't have batted an eyelash at the bouncing up and down. But with the Freefighters, who weren't quite used to the ride, their legs and butts were sore, as if they'd been bouncing on porcupine quills. Everything below the waist felt as if it were on fire to Rockson.

It took another half hour or so for them to reach the rear defensive units of Tutankhamen's slowly moving army. They related the bad news to the army's outpost men, who were sitting atop four heavily armored elephants, and were told the general was three miles ahead at the lead of the army.

They shot off alongside the outpost men's beasts, and soon found the main body of the army.

The elephants were heavy-laden, their packs loaded down with all the various forms of smaller lasers that the fighters possessed, and mucho supplies. Women and children rode in the center, the most protected part of the migration.

"Rockson, Rahallah—you are safe," Tutankhamen said when he saw them ride up. Tutankhamen rode in the very forefront of the army with his top ten generals on elephants around him, so they could confer and make plans while in motion.

"Yes, but Sesostris is dead," Rockson yelled back as Chen brought their war bull to an even pace alongside the general. "And—and—" he could hardly bring himself to say it. "And Killov has all the goddamn sticks now—the Qu'ul and the Ra."

Tutankhamen's face went pale. "Then we are doomed," the Great Pharaoh said, his words slow and terribly sad. "All our people—you as well. Probably the whole planet within another year or two. Everything will be gone. We have failed. Failed ourselves—and failed the living gods."

"Not so fast, chief," Rockson said, jumping up so he was balancing on the middle of the war platform. "Let's see if we can't have a little powwow and figure this whole stinking thing out." He stepped over until he was on the edge of his elephant, and suddenly leaped out, jumping across a good six feet to the side of Tutankhamen's bull.

Two of his guards, armed with long razor-edged swords, looked a little nervous as there had been assassination attempts over the years. But Rockson smiled and raised his hands to show he had nothing bad in mind. He sat down quickly in the extra-wide battle station that was the pharaoh's. This one was a good eight feet on a side, extending out over the sides of the elephant. Inside it was a priceless carpet and silk pillows to lie on. Now this was more like it,

Rockson decided on the spot.

"Have you a map?" Rock asked.

"Yes! I was just going over this map," Tutankhamen said, pointing to a spread-out sheet of papyrus in the middle of his finely woven rug. The paper had its own glow, as the tomb did. "You see, we're here." He swept his finger along the Nile, indicating their position near it.

Rock pointed too. "They're back about here," he said, pointing to a spot a good foot behind them on the map. "I would estimate about twenty miles off, moving at approximately twelve miles an hour, hopefully not this way. They might not be aware of us—maybe!"

Rockson looked at the map, getting a sense of where they were, the scale of things. If only he had done this before!

The pharaoh said, "We can travel maybe another hundred miles and then—it will become much slower for the bulls as they are heavy burdened, plus there are thick, pointed rocks everywhere along the riverbanks. Ordinarily the bulls can handle rocks and stones, but these are known as the spear stones— because of their extremely sharp tips. It gets worse the farther you get in. I want to get there and maybe have a few days to figure out some strategy. It is a defendable area."

"What's this here?" Rockson asked, pointing to a large shape jutting right across the river.

"The Aswan Dam," Tutankhamen replied. "An immense dam made of concrete thicker than the Great Pyramid. It was built before the Great Nuke War."

"Does it still work—I mean, hold water, whatever, behind it?"

"Yes—much water. A vast Nile-fed lake," Tutankhamen replied. "Often my people have fished from the reservoir of water above it. We call it Umm Durmankh. I have floated on its placid surface, in better days. Yes—it is filled with water, billions upon countless billions of gallons."

"Then I'm getting a crazy idea," Rock said as he stroked his forehead nervously, almost afraid to propose the thought.

"Well, let me hear it," Tutankhamen said, leaning back on the side of the platform against several pillows. "My generals and I haven't been coming up with anything—anything that would really stop them. After the reports of their ability to kill such huge numbers of men and even war bulls so easily—I can't pretend that we can use our usual tactics. They would be useless."

"That's exactly it, Your Greatness," Rockson said as their bull suddenly jumped up right over a fallen cypress tree. Rock felt his stomach turn over a few times as they soared a good twelve feet through the air, though Tutankhamen didn't seem to notice. But then he'd been born and bred on these damned things. "We can't face them directly," Rock continued. "As powerful as your lasers are, they're just no match for falling mountains. But what if—what if somehow we could lure them into this lower valley below the Aswan Dam. And then—using the war bulls' combined laser power—crack open the dam and send all that water down on the Killovian forces. Like Old Moses and the Red Sea. We'll smack it down on them like a tidal wave. They have rocks, we have water!"

"It's—I—" the pharaoh seemed genuinely nonplussed by the idea—not even sure whether it was insane or the best concept of the last hundred years. It was an awesome idea, and his brain tried to expand to envelop it.

"Yes, I suppose the combined power of all our lasers might break the shell of concrete that holds back the water. It's all theoretically possible I would imagine. But—"

"Yeah, I know. But. I feel the same way," Rock said. "But we know for sure what's going to happen if we don't get something spectacular to match their firepower. It's like, as far as I can see, we've got nothing to lose."

"Oh, great Isis," Tutankhamen said, raising his arms high to the streaked dawn. "Send me a sign. Tell us of your wishes." As Rockson looked on—and, from their elephant, Chen and Rahallah as well—a single meteor streaked suddenly across the sky, much brighter than the fading pinpoints of the stars. It rode for a full four seconds, streaking blue and white and then red. Then it was gone.

"Red, white, blue!" the general shouted. "Like *your* flag! The gods have spoken," Tutankhamen yelled excitedly, turning around as he addressed the generals via a handspeaker. They listened with growing amazement.

"To Aswan. To Aswan, our entire army—where the final battle of Egypt will be fought. One way or another," the leader shouted, "whether we live or die—whether we win or not, we are fighting the holy war. The war of Isis and Ra." Tutankhamen raised his battle sword high, and the first real rays of the sun bounced off it. The generals around his battle elephant raised their two-pronged spears and cheered, stabbing them in the air. The war bulls began moving forward at increased speed, so that within minutes they were traveling at full gallop heading

214

straight for the Aswan. And as they rode the riders on them sang. To Rockson it sounded like:

Weride to death. To death we ride.
We shall live and our enemy die.
Or we shall die and our enemy live.
But we fight the battle of Isis and Ra.
And we ride to death, we ride to death.

CHAPTER TWENTY-SIX

It was a tremendous strategic question: how best to blow the damned thing up. And how to lure Killov and his forces right into the path of the great wave that would come down the lower Aswan Valley from the burst Aswan dam. If it did burst. And how to survive it all themselves.

Rock and Tutankhamen, Chen, Rahallah, and all ten of the pharaoh's generals all shouted ideas and battle plans back and forth. Until at last, as they came to within about ten miles of the dam, they all agreed.

They saw it now, as they came around a curve in the river, rising like some manmade mountain ahead, curving all the way across the mile-wide river, storing up its immense liquid power on the other side of titanic concrete walls.

Rock and his men and about a third of the elephants headed across to the other side of the river via the wide road on the top of the dam. Tutankhamen led the other two thirds of the army along the side they were on. Another hundred of the fastest war bulls, ridden by volunteer relatives of Sesostris, were the bait to pull the Army of Amun straight into the lower Aswan Valley, where they would be in the path of the bursting tidal wave. Or so it went on paper.

Rockson was glad to be back on Kral. The beast had made its way back across the desert, following some super-homing instinct!

Once across the Nile, Rock could see Tutankhamen's bulls setting up into long triple lines along a concrete roadway that ran right up the side of the steep hill on the west side of the Aswan Dam. That road had been built up heavily to take even big service vehicles. There were walkways and multi-layered levels everywhere. Tutankhamen stood on his elephant, screaming out directions to his troops through his handspeaker. The man had a booming voice, and it carried down over the whole valley, echoing back and forth across the face of the dam so even Rock could hear it on the wind from over a mile away.

Rock pulled out the old binocs that the elephant generals had dug up for him. They were rusted, with U.S. Army markings on them, so Rock knew they were at least a century old. But then the United States had been supplying the Egyptian Army with weapons and military supplies for years before the conflagration. And now they had come full circle back to him, an American. He focused the glasses downriver as his elephant trudged ahead, one step after another as the rocky slope got steeper.

Rockson could see the whole thing, as if it was some kind of miniature battle scene made out of clay, far below him. The valley opening out as the mountains on each side slowly slanted downward as they drew away from the dam. The Nile extended far to the north. A band of green ran along each side. And there, about three miles off, the bait to lure Killov—the elephant force, racing with everything it had back up the valley along the side of the river.

As Rockson raised the glasses a little more, he heard a sudden, terrible roar as a piece of rock the size of a subway car came slamming down on three or four of the spread-out bait-squad. *Too soon!*

When it rose up, there was just red and splintered bone where the beasts and men had been. All along the field of his glasses the enemy was coming down the valley from both sides—on camel, on foot, even a contingent on some sort of levitated raft! But it was the ones in the very forefront, the first ranks of the moving camels, the riders holding the red anti-grav sticks, that Rock was interested in.

He focused the glasses for a second, and thought he spotted Killov as a peaked hood fell from a gaunt, pale face. He swore he saw the Skull staring back up at him and pointing a Qu'ul!

At that very instant a huge boulder came down just yards from some of the other bait-riders, this group more fortunately situated.

The Amun priests tried again. They quickly sent more boulders slamming down onto the lure site. Others saw that there was something going on the slopes of each side of the dam. Huge slabs came flying through the sky, shooting up toward the ranks of war bulls on each side of the dam that were filling every bit of stone or cement walkway that could be found.

Rock waited as planned, though it was agonizingly hard to. They had to sucker the Killov forces into the valley, get them in trouble as much as possible. Get them close to the dam, so there would be no way out, no way they'd miss the brunt of the crashing sea of water.

But suddenly, waiting wasn't possible any longer. Boulders began coming down on both sides of the river, slamming into the elephants on Rock's flank and on the far side as well. It was as if thunder was going off in their very midst. Suddenly, ahead of time, Tutankhamen's forces were shooting up at the dam. The elephants all raised their trunks and fired out the laser rays' blue and red, snapping with electric energy.

Rockson gave his beast the kick signal for aiming and firing, and it raised its long trunk as well. The laser apparatus came whirring out of the snout, and began glowing and blinking a deep violet color. The elephants behind Kral followed suit, as the whole slope of war bulls with riders all over their backs raised their trunks and the laser weapons emerged.

The whole contingent of laser-equipped pachyderms shot, and a thousand beams of the most aching blue the world had ever seen came instantaneously out of them. Unlike bullets, the laser wave didn't take time. It just was there. Between the Tutankhamen forces on both sides of the Nile, there were literally thousands of the crackling rays playing over the surface of the dam. It all didn't seem to be doing a damn thing, though. They had to concentrate the beams more accurately, Rock suddenly realized, bring all the power to an exact focus.

"Fire exactly where I'm firing," Rock screamed out over one of the Egyptian handspeakers. The word was passed down the line and within seconds, more and more of the blue beams were snapping into the same spot—just about dead center on the dam, the spot where Rockson figured the greatest weight of water would be pressing in from the other side. The spot in a dam that Rocky Mountain beavers always fortified!

Across the Nile, Tutankhamen saw what Rock had

in mind, and commanded his forces to do the same. Killov's forces were right down the river, just five hundred yards off, closing in on the sacrifice-force tearing along just in front of them.

The concrete in the dead center of the dam began to glow—first orange, then white. It takes a lot of heat to make concrete melt, but the combined strength of 3,000 beams of laser energy was like a controlled thermonuclear explosion.

Suddenly the circle of heat was a good twenty feet wide and almost blue like the laser beams themselves. There was a roar, even louder than the slamming rocks of the Amun Army rising and falling all around them now and creating mega-death through their ranks. All the men looked up as the spot that had been glowing erupted out of the face of the dam like a lava explosion, red hot and melting.

A burst of water came shooting out behind the spewing concrete pieces, under incredible pressure as it rushed through the circular twenty-foot hole. And even as the elephants were commanded to shut off their lasers, their riders gazed up to see the Nile's immense water pressure eating at the edges of the rapidly expanding hole.

It was like a domino effect—but very fast. The circle of exploding concrete spread, moving out on all sides as the water bit away at the ninety-foot-thick cement dam at the rate of about five-hundred feet a second. And the more water that roared out in a waterfall dwarfing Niagara itself, the bigger the hole became. Suddenly the whole center of the Aswan went with a roar that took out over a billion tons of concrete in an instant, sending it flying through the air, straight down at the advancing Killovian forces and the heroic, doomed remnant of the bait-squad.

But the concrete shrapnel was the least of their worries. For right behind it was a wall of water as high as an eighty-story building as half the liquid contents of the multi-trillion-gallon reservoir that the dam had contained came out in the space of seconds.

The wave roared out into the air like a thing alive, a twisting maelstrom of liquid which just seemed to expand out in every direction as it flew. Rock could see right away that it was going to take out some of the main force's elephants too. Those who were on the lower rock ledges or concrete walkways across river below five hundred feet elevation might be in trouble.

Five hundred yards down the river, the army of Killov saw the great wall of blue water right overhead and realized they'd been trapped. But there wasn't a hell of a lot they could do beyond point with their power-sticks around in the air. It's hard to push back water. Liquids are tricky. And they only had about two seconds to learn how. For suddenly, the tidal wave which had flown out a good two thousand feet from the face of the high dam came down in one immense wall a half mile on a side. It crashed with the loudest sound Rock had ever heard, making his eardrums vibrate like rubber bands. Heroes and villains, everyone and everything in the flood's path instantly disappeared beneath the crushing waters.

On both sides of the Nile, spreading back a mile, camels, riders, and thousands of infantry died as the water crashed down. And it was far bigger slaughter than any of the mountains the Skull-man had raised up to kill. They all just vanished beneath the churning foam and twisting blackness. Their anti-grav sticks were sucked down, and boulders everywhere

221

dropped from the sky as they regained their full weight, bounding down the slopes into the churning madness.

The waters took all of it down. Took them all as Moses had commanded the Red Sea to take the pharaoh's chariots. Of such things are legends born.

CHAPTER TWENTY-SEVEN

The raging water released by the dam continued to churn debris downriver like clothes in a washing machine. The currents put in play by the super-tonnage of water rushed from bank to bank with bubbles and whitewater everywhere. Dead camels, troops of Killov's army, a high priest here and there, white robe billowing out in the water—all floated by, bobbing up and down, spinning around in the mud-black river. A river of the doomed.

Already vultures roamed high in the sky in great arcing circles, slowly swooping lower down as the vanquished began rolling up onto the shores of the Nile, snagging among the weeds, dragging onto stumps that jutted out. Crocodiles, vultures, ants, bugs, and beetles of every size and description began feeding on them. Taking what was now theirs.

In the midst of it all, a small figure floated half submerged alongside a dead bloated camel. His gaunt face was hidden in the black waters that swirled around the slowly turning beast whose white stomach was distorted and had risen up like dough in the oven. The submerged figure's eyes darted back and forth, continuously raking the waters for crocodiles. In one hand he held a length of broken sword by the dull end of the blade. The other hand clutched the soaked, thick hairy hide of the bloated animal's side, pressing close against the camel so he couldn't be seen. Colonel Killov kicked slowly to keep from going under as he floated along, dead center in the river, only occasionally allowing his mouth to reach the surface and suck in air.

As he floated, he cursed silently. He had been so close. He had had both sides of the power spectrum in his grasp. His armies were poised to sweep all of Africa. And then . . . Total and complete annihilation!

He would devote the rest of his life to taking out Rockson. Nothing else mattered now. Nothing.

And suddenly, from the pits of the darkest depression the skull-faced KGB butcher had ever known, he was released. He felt risen up into a kind of mad elation. An elation of revenge. And he began planning how he would kill him. Would he strangle him? Pour acid on him? Oh, the many ways that Ted Rockson could die! And in a bizarre way, Killov almost felt sort of happy as he fended off crocs and lashed out at vultures that swung too low. As his dead camel slowly spun down the endless black Nile, he realized that he had a reason to live.